The Fiction Of Marlon

I hope you enjoy these short stories!

~ Marlon

By Marlon Pearson

Acknowledgements

I remember years ago watching a late night talk show. I don't remember the host. I don't remember any of the guests except for Joe Walsh. He was the musical guest for the night. Before he started into his first song he made a dedication that has stuck with me all these years. He said "I'd like to dedicate this song to all the people who have never had a song dedicated to them." I think that is the coolest dedication ever because it had the chance to make so many people feel good. All the people, including me, who never had a song dedicated to them got that song that night. Maybe I'm taking my own experience and projecting it out to the rest of the audience, but Joe's dedication really was a 'feel good' dedication. At least it made me feel good, and I hope it made others feel good, too.

I believe Joe went on to sing "Life's Been Good". I don't have a Maserati that does 185, but my life has been good so far. Along the way there have been plenty of people who have encouraged and supported me. P.A., you are a constant source of encouragement, support and inspiration. Your shine always warms my life. Manual, Bob, and ZZ; thanks for being my captive audience during our drives to Lake Tahoe and those pizza and movie nights. You guys always listened to my story ideas and gave me your honest feedback and opinions. That's what friends are supposed to do. I thank all of you.

While I don't want to duplicate Joe's exact dedication, I do want to try to share that same spirit with all of you. This book is a collection of my short stories. They are fictional slice-of-life tales I hope you will find entertaining and interesting. Each story stands on its own, with a unique narrator each time. I hope they give you a life-is-good feeling. Please enjoy them.

More of my work can be found at http://www.tfom.net
Regards,
-Marlon Pearson

Table of Contents

Biscuits

Some people look at my dog and they are appalled by his fatness. I admit he is a happy fat dog, but he does get walked. He gets some agility training, too. But he never ever gets 'dog food'. As long as I have lived on my own, I've had my dog, but never have I allowed dog food in my house. Human food is all we eat. It's a health issue.

I don't go to the pet store. I don't even go down the pet food isle at the grocery store. There's a pet food smell that permeates all of it, and I never want to experience that smell again.

Back when I was young, too young to look beyond my own adoration for my parents, they took advantage of me in a sick, sick fashion. They look back at it and laugh. They call it harmless fun, but I ask you to be the judge.

Back then, a fun Saturday morning for us was a trip to the local farm and feed store. My dad worked there and it was such a great adventure to walk in, holding his hand and mom's hand, too. The workers always gave us a warm welcome, waving to dad, smiling at mom, and commenting on how much I'd grown since the last Saturday visit. It was the excitement of being a young family on an adventure together.

The feed and farm store was huge, with a two-story tall ceiling. It had rows and rows of barn supplies and animal feed. There was a smell of hay and earth throughout the place. Up in the rafters, small groups of Chickadees cheerfully raced from beam to beam. It was the place I learned to count up to five. Dad would start me with row one and go up to row five, not just counting, but also explaining the stock of each row. Row one held nails and screws; row two contained hinges and brackets. Dad said rows three and four were for the cowboys. Three had all sizes of ropes, along with bridles and leather gloves. Row four had saddle goods and accessories. Five had canine treats and toys.

Maybe it was my fault. Mom says I was pretending to be a dog. Don't all kids do that? She says we were walking down row five and when I noticed all the puppies and pooches on the boxes and bags, I got down on my hands and knees. I started barking and panting.

"Oh...what a cute puppy" she said.

I barked.

"I bet you're a good little puppy" she replied.

As she grabbed a chew toy off the shelf, she asked "How about a toy, puppy?" I shook my head 'no' and barked. She grabbed another one, "How about this one?" I barked 'no' again. She paused and looked around.

"Hmmm...how about a treat?"

Who says no to a treat? So while I was enthusiastically barking and spinning around in anticipation of my treat, she grabbed and opened a box of Kennel Corner's Better Biscuits. I stopped spinning when I saw she held a treat in her hand. Still playing the dog, I barked and begged. She gave me my first, but not last, dog biscuit. It was dry and crunchy and not at all sweet. Looking back, it really wasn't much of a treat. Mom patted me on the head, and as dad came around the corner and down the aisle, mom told me to stand up, then she closed up the box and put it back on the shelf.

For the next two years, we made many of our Saturdays special by going to dad's workplace. Even though Saturday was dad's day off, he sometimes would help customers, folks that he knew. If he went off with the customer, mom and I would usually find our way to row five. When I was a good puppy, I'd get a treat. It wasn't always Kennel Corner biscuits. Sometimes it was Alpo Tasty Treats or Furminator Dog Bites. Once it was Mr. Eds Natural Biscuits. I actually gagged on one of those. Good thing, too, because I later found out they contained horse parts.

I cried on the Saturday morning I found out my dad had changed jobs and we would not be going on our adventures anymore. Mom must have suspected my devastation because after she dried my tears, from her apron pocket she pulled one last treat. I wanted to wolf it down in anger, but I knew it really was my last treat so I had better savor it, just nibble away at it. Plus, I knew very well that those biscuits were dirt-clod hard and too dry to take in big bites.

I had completely forgotten all of this until I moved out on my own. At 23, I had just started renting one side of a duplex. One evening after work, I was out front watering the lawn. A stray dog, a very scruffy looking Spaniel and something mix, came trotting down the block. I watched him as he went past tree after tree without stopping. When he got to my driveway, he sat down right in front of me. He looked up at me and tilted his head as if I'd just said 'hippopotamus". I asked him if he was hungry. He sure looked it. He barked and spun around in a circle. Without really thinking, I said "Oh what a cute puppy. I bet you want a treat!"

That broke it for me. Memories of the feed and farm supply store raced into my mind. My mouth went dog-biscuit dry and I may have let out a little yelp. In an instant, I knew I wasn't ever going to give him or any other dog of mine a "treat". I marched into the kitchen and from the refrigerator I grabbed an unopened package of Kraft American Cheese Singles, a 16 pack. On my way back out the front, I went through the garage and picked up my new lawn chair. At the driveway, I snapped it open and plopped down in it. With a glutinous resolve, I tore open the cheese pack. My new dog, "Scotty", and I easily made our way through that pack of 16, and we've lived happily off human food ever since. It's a health issue. A mental health issue.

Saving The Earth

There's a place just east of Bakersfield, California called Weedpatch. A man-made irrigation canal runs through the eastern part of Weedpatch. On the south side of the canal there is a pheasant farm. It sits amongst small, dusty houses and unpaved roads.

In the spring time, around Easter, kids will walk along the canal's south bank. They'll bomb the canal's tadpoles with dirt clods, but they'll leave the regal birds alone. They'll swat at dragonflies and dance around bees, but the corralled fowl will remain unharassed and mostly ignored. When an Airforce jet flies low overhead and blocks out all other sound, the kids stop and the adolescent amphibians get a chance to regroup at the water's edge as the ripples dissipate. The pheasants don't notice a thing.

Downstream is a grate across the canal and things get caught in it. Not strange things, but strange in the water. Why is there a cowboy shirt, with three pearl snaps on the sleeve, in the water? A thermos cap jitters between two teeth of the grate, but can't make it past either one. Rumors of a large catfish, idle and indifferent, waiting at the base of the grate, always are discussed amongst the children because their dads talk about it, too.

Across the water, on the remote, untouched northern side, corn stocks, short and green, are two to four inches out of the rowed ground and no human is ever seen over there.

"It's the moon over there", one kid says. "And this is the earth. Let's bomb It", someone shouts as he reaches for a dirt clod. "Let's nuke it", another shouts. Soon, their side of the canal is barren of loose rock and dirt, all launched to save the earth.

Saving the earth is what was done back then, back when kids played.

A February Sunday in Milpitas

It's that California Sunday when the cherry blossoms suddenly appear, brilliantly white, obnoxious and jubilant. Their overnight usurpation of the starkly winter-aged and weather worn tree branches is complete. In this morning's bright, breezy sunlight they celebrate their victory like Mardi Gras party goers crowding the streets on Fat Tuesday. The wind gives their celebration a swaying, undulating motion while the attending honey bees and hummingbirds provide a subdued soundtrack, just audible as my dog and I walk past their vibrant merriment.

The two trees in my neighbor's front yard are in full bloom, as is the solo tree we pass a few minutes later while we continue on our normal Sunday trek.

When we turn from our residential street to the busier boulevard, I see the same Big Whitey's shopping cart I saw last Sunday. Its right front wheel is still pinned under the lower support brace of the 46 bus stop bench. I wonder if the Whitey's coupon flyer from last week has survived these last 7 days. Something flutters in the cart's basket but I'm not yet close enough to see what it actually is.

Before Jace and I can get to the bus stop, a dull black compact pickup truck, pulling a long, flatbed trailer, rattles to a stop just past the bus stop bench. Seeing the pickup halt in the bus zone, I immediately stop and think "That's illegal. You can't park at a bus stop". Then I notice the rattling noise was from a dozen or so shopping carts already harvested and stationed on the flatbed trailer. The truck driver has set the hazards lights to flashing.

Two slight, tattooed youths rise up from their riding stations in the back of the truck and make the jump directly onto the flatbed dory. They surround a mechanical contraption situated at the front of the trailer. This thing has a stout post coming up from the trailer bed to about waist height. On top of the post is some type of wheel or spool with a coil of wire rope wrapped around it. Off the wheel there is a 24 inch arm sticking out towards the back of the trailer. A handle is connected to the wheel, too.

While the first youth addresses the mechanism, the second goes to the back of the trailer and kicks a lever that drops the trailer's tailgate to make a ramp. The second one checks the security of the wrangled carts as he walks back to the front of the trailer to wait on his companion, who is still bent over the mechanism. I didn't see it, but the first youth must have released some lock on the wheel because he straightens up and steps back. The second youth is now pulling the wire rope out from the wheel, first he feeds it through the ringlets on the mechanism's arm and then he walks with it to the back of the trailer. The mechanism's handle spins as the rope and the second youth make their way to the back of the trailer. He stops at the edge of the trailer. He doesn't get out of it.

The shopping cart is just a few feet away, but instead of walking to it and hooking on the rope, the youth stays onboard. He pulls more rope and coils it at his feet. Now he has the end of the rope in his right hand. When he raises his arm, I see there is a stiff lead on the rope end. The lead is just about 2 feet long. It looks like a mini javelin, with a small arrowhead tip.

He pulls his arm back, pauses for aim, then shoots the javelin right through the plastic lattice of the front of the Big Whitey cart. It's an easy target and he has a direct hit on the first try. He grabs the wire rope and starts to pull it in. At the same time, the first youth has started to work the mechanism's handle. Once the slack is gone from the rope, youth-two lets go and moves out of the way.

Whitey's cart doesn't put up much fight as youth-one works the handle to reel it in. He pulls it free of the bench brace. Once the cart is free of the bench, youth-one stops cranking and the other youth grabs the wire cable that is now stretched tight between the mechanism and the cart. He walks along the trailer's back edge towards the street side of the trailer, taking the cable with him. His pulling of the wire rope causes the cart to angle off the sidewalk and towards the street. He continues to pull the cable until the cart has dropped off the curb and is in the street. Youth-two let's go of the rope and signals to Youth-One. With the cart in the street, One starts reeling it in towards the trailer. This all seems well practiced.

One quickly has the cart at the edge of the ramp, but then the cart stops. Surely it is supposed to just go up the ramp and onto the trailer, where it will be subdued by these youths. Something else has happened, the cart is not complying.

After a couple failed attempts to crank forward, One cranks the handle backwards to loosen the rope. He yells

"Ishmael, what's wrong back there?"

"Come take a look, Kwee." is the reply from Two. Jace and I take that as an invitation to move a bit closer, too.

One sees the same thing I do. When the tailgate was dropped to make a ramp, it didn't lay flat on the road. Because the back of the trailer was pointed slightly in towards the sidewalk, instead of being parallel to it, part of the lip of the tailgate landed on the curb. This left part of the tailgate up off the road. From where Jace and I stand, a few steps behind the trailer, we can see the right triangle that was created by the mishap. The roadway is the base of the triangle, the curb is the short perpendicular piece and the ramp is the hypotenuse, running from the top of the curb to the road's asphalt some 5 feet out from the curb.

Like most grocery shopping carts, Whitey's carts have a lower frame, a lower lip, where shoppers can place heavy or bulky items. When One pulled the cart towards the tailgate, the gate was just high enough off the road for the cart's lower lip to slide under the tailgate. It looks as if Whitey's shopping cart is attacking the trailer. It appears that Whitey is taking a big bite out of the trailer's tailgate.

One inspects the situation for another couple seconds, then he speaks to Two and points to a spot in the back of the truck. Two nods and hustles to that spot, jumping back across the divide to the truck bed. He bends down and comes up with a long, hooked pole. A fisherman's gaff is in his hand. He looks at One, who quickly nods. Two hustles to rejoin One. Together they use the gaff to push Big Whitey's cart back and free of the ramp, again being careful not to fall out of the trailer.

One heads back to the mechanism while Two continues to work the gaff. Next, Two gaffs Big Whitey's lower lip and begins to lift the beast up onto the ramp. Two's feet are planted far apart. In his right hand he has the end of the gaff, with his knuckles tucked into his hip. His left elbow is stuck into his gut and his left hand grips the gaff about three feet from his right hand hold. He starts to lean back and lift. I can see the gaff bending under the massive weight of Big Whitey. The front wheels reluctantly come up off the sea of asphalt.

Two continues to lift it, but he also pulls the gaff in towards himself, bringing the cart closer while raising the front. The cart is tilted at an angle that is akin to when an ocean dwelling mammal breaches the liquid surface.

"Thar she blows!" I shout jovially and then glance at Two, Ishmael, for a reaction.

He slowly shakes his head side to side. It's an "Oh, brother" shake, but he says nothing and keeps on task.

The wheels are well above the ramp when Two half turns to One and yells "Alright". One gets cranking on the mechanism. As the carcass is brought on board, Two removes the gaff from lower lip and then skillfully sinks it into the back of the beast, where he uses it to lift the back wheels up over the void and onto the ramp. One and Two have complete control over Big Whitey and skillfully maneuver it the rest of the way up the ramp and then in line with what they've already harvested. Two sets the gaff down so he can unhook the rope.

As One and Two begin to tie down Big Whitey's cart, Jace and I decide it's time to continue our morning trek. We slowly walk by the bus bench and are alongside the trailer as they finish securing the wheeled thing. We watch as Two raises the tailgate and engages the lever to hold the gate in position. At the same time, One goes and reels in the last bit of rope and then bends over the mechanism, presumably to engage the same hidden clasp he initially used to free the rope. Two picks up the gaff and joins One at the front of the trailer. One, then Two, deftly jump back into the pickup bed. Two quickly returns the gaff to someplace in the truck bed. By the time they are in their seats, we are nearly at the cab of the truck. The captain has started up the truck and when One taps on the roof, the anchor is lifted and they set sail.

As they lurch away from the bus stop, out of the driver's window emerges a pale hand with gnarled, boney fingers, followed by an arm inside the sleeve of a dark blue pea coat. As the hand and arm are extending out from the window, the palm is up, as if to check for rain. When the arm is about two thirds out of the window, it stops extending. The palm rotates until it faces down. The arm bends at the elbow until the palm is against the outside of the truck door. The hand moves in a slow, caressing circle over a discolored area of the truck door. The palm does a second and a third circle over the area. There's a formality about these movements that is reinforced when at the end of the third circle the arm is straighten back out, the palm is rotated back to facing upward and then arm and hand are retracted back into the truck.

Naturally, my eyes are drawn to this love zone on the truck door. Before the truck can get up to full speed, I am just able to see the object of the captain's affection. It's a bit faded, but I can tell it is a round decal about 14 inches in diameter. In the center is an image of a lad harpooning a shopping cart. There is some block lettering around the perimeter of the decal. I have to hurry to read it. I quickly go around the lettering once to find the spacing and word breaks. The truck is pulling away but I have enough time to make a second pass. I read it out loud

"A. Hab's Cart Retrieval and Rendering Service".

I look to Jace, who's busily inspecting the bus stop sign post, and I say "A. Hab? Captain A. Hab ?". Jace has no answer for me.

He makes the post his and we move on. It's just another two blocks east before the boulevard reaches the foothills. There's a four way stop, with the north-south road crossing the boulevard. At the base of the foothill intersection we take a right and head south. This is my favorite part of the walk because there's very little car traffic and with the foothills on our left it feels more remote and rural than it really is. There are a few family farms and some abandoned fruit and nut orchards spread across the apron of these rolling hills. Sometimes I see wild turkeys or deer in the orchards. Twice I've seen coyotes higher up the hills.

Jace and I walk quietly for a couple miles, eventually turning back into the residential area. We return home just in time for lunch. Lunch is simple and easy. A tuna sandwich, chips, baby carrots and a High Life do the trick for me. Jace gets a half scoop of kibbles and bits and a dish of fresh water.

Our afternoon habit on nice Sundays such as today is to retire to the garage and contemplate the beauty of life. I open up the garage car door, then clip Jace's collar onto his garage leash and I set up my lawn chair. From our station we can see up and down the block and to the east, above the rooftops of our across-the-street neighbors we can see the upper region of the same grassy foothills along with the wonderfully blue February sky that we saw on our walk. We sit easy and watch the afternoon slowly arrive.

Later on, Jace barks me awake. As I look around my world I see something that reminds me it's that special time of year when the deaf kids and the old, hard-of-hearing folks like me have an afternoon chance. Even if we can't hear the worn out melodies of "Pop goes the weasel" or "It's a small world" announcing the impending drive-by of Perez's ice cream and salty-sweet motor-powered snackatorium , we have a visual cue that gives us a chance to call him to heel.

In particular, the local ravens have come to understand the ways and means of Perez and his converted postal truck. For over 20 years, from the day after Epiphany to the day before Christmas, Perez has driven the same route, with the same converted all-metal US Postal truck, and, as far as I can tell, the same two song play list.

Here in Milpitas, February is when leftover walnuts from the nearby abandoned orchards are ready for easy picking and all the ravens have come to know it. The young ravens will try to crack the nuts simple by dropping them in the road. They'll pull a nut from the tree, fly to a nearby streetlight and from that perch they will drop the nut onto the road, hoping gravity will do the job. I've seen it take as many as ten tries, ten drops, before a nut cracks.

The older, wiser ravens have a much better system. They go pull the nuts off the unattended trees, fly high overhead to spy the Perezmobile, and then dart down in front of it and lay their nuts out on the road. On a clear, sunny day like today it is somewhat mesmerizing to watch.

Image this sequence. You're looking out over the neighborhood roof tops. From beyond the local rooftops, a raven shoots up in the air, hangs there for a few seconds, then darts down towards some nearby neighborhood. Then another raven does the same, but this one darts down a little closer to your neighborhood.

You know what's coming. You start thinking about the Mint Chocolate It's Its or the ice cream drumstick headed your way so you go get your buck fifty and watch the ravens get closer and closer. Here's Perez turning onto your street and at the same time you see raven after raven setting uncracked walnuts in front of his vehicle. Perez seems oblivious to the ravens, but he somehow hits every single nut in the road. He's like an old magician doing card tricks for the thousandth time. While he drives, he doesn't even think about the nuts. He just nails them.

The ravens lay the whole, uncracked nuts in front of Perez like believers with offerings to their savior, then after he has passed, they jump at the opened, exposed manna he has delivered unto them. Us hard of hearing know the swooping ravens signal our opportunity for an afternoon repast, a delight, a snack of our choice, from the Perezmeister.

From my lawn chair in the garage I wave him down. I get up and grab a handful of coins from the change-jar I keep on the workbench. I watch as he stops on the far side of the street, but right in front of my driveway. He's a good man. When he stops, three ravens, each with a walnut in its beak, come to rest on the Perezmobile roof. Jace guards the house while I go visit with Perez and his ravens.

With his Real Madrid soccer shirt on, it is easy to talk with Perez, I just ask him about his team. While he fishes around in the freezer for my It's It he updates me on the latest news. Apparently a nearly blind linesman missed an offsides call that cost Real Madrid their last game. I tell him "Man, bad officiating sucks. That's the worst way to lose. Do you think it will happen to your team again?"

Up on the Perezmobile metal roof, one of the ravens must have grown impatient waiting for Perez to get going again because there's a tapping, gently rapping right above the driver side door. Perez pauses to give my question serious consideration. After a few seconds, he shakes his head no and answers my question with "No, nevermore, nevermore".

His answer causes us both to pause. Shortly, we hear it again, the tapping, somewhat louder than before. As I start to ask him about his sometimes girlfriend, Lenore, another raven lands on the roof. Perez and I hear Jace bark at us. "You know what he wants" I say. Perez asks "Chicarones?" I nod. He sets Jace's bag of fried pork bellies and my plastic wrapped mint-flavored chocolate dipped ice cream cookie sandwich on the window sill. "Two fifty" he says. "That is such a deal" I reply. He chuckles, I pay and pick up my winnings. "See ya next time, Perez" I say.

As I walk back to the garage I see the two kids from next door, Max and Min, come rushing out their front door. Max pushes the spring loaded screen door wide open so they both make it out, but right after Min is past it, it bangs closed. The kids have their sights set on Perez.

"Wait Perez ! wait!!" they yell in unison even though he hasn't moved.

They each do a quick glance-glance to check the street is clear enough to dart over to Perez's window on the street side of his vehicle. They get there safely and begin bouncing in front of his window, scanning all the colorful ice cream and popsicle choices displayed around Perez's serving window. I don't hear what they order, but Perez has them setup quickly. They grab their selections and, after another quick glance-glance, dash back home.

"Mom, can we eat them now ?" I hear Max ask as he disappears through the front screen door. Min is right behind him with "Pleaseeee?" Their screen door bangs again, followed by the sound of their front door closing, too. The kids go in and out often enough and loud enough that I know the sounds, same as I know the sounds of my own front and screen doors. Perez starts up his vehicle and heads on down the block. The roof top ravens take flight and then start swooping down in front of his truck.

Now I'm in my chair with my It's It and it's goodness. I've opened Jace's bag of deep fried pork bellies. Between my bites of It's It, I throw Jace pieces of his chicharones. Most of them he snatches right out of midair. A few bounce off his bite attempt and he has to chase them down. It's Sunday afternoon so we take our time and enjoy our snacks. After we finish, I take the wrapper and empty bag to the trash, then go inside to get a sweater and the Harlan Coben book I started last Sunday.

When I get back to my chair in the garage, I see Jace is sleeping on his rug next to my chair. The kids are back outside and racing up and down the sidewalk on their rollerblades. Their dog, a friendly, intelligent, protective mongrel, is out there with them. As Max zooms by he calls out "Hi Jace. Hi Mr. P." Jace sleeps, I wave. Min is next with

"Hey Jace. Hey Mr. P". I wave to Min. Last comes their dog, Coco. She trots along behind the kids, her kids.

The kids' playzone extends just 2 houses on either side of their home so while they burn off their sugar rush they will be zipping back and forth past my driveway about 18 times a minute. On their next zip past my driveway I notice Coco is carrying a small, grayish, disk in her mouth. Curious about it, I call her over. Of course, the kids keep skating but Coco comes to me. I pet her a couple times on the head and then take a closer look at what she's carrying. It's a rice cake. I tell her "Eat it, girl, eat it". She tilts her head to one side and gives that confused you-don't-make-sense dog look. I go to reach for the rice cake and she jumps back in a playful way.

Just then, Min comes back by so I tell her Coco has a rice cake. Min slows down, glances at Coco and answers "Yea, she likes to bury them in mom's flower bed." "Does she ever eat them?" I ask. Min replies "No, I don't think so" and takes off to catch up with her brother who just went by.

I look back at Coco and she is watching and waiting. I call her over again and manage to get the cake, intact, from her. She backs up and starts barking at me. I know she is a Frisbee dog and loves to play fetch with a tennis ball, too. I wonder how well the rice cake would fly.

I remember the one time I tried a rice cake. It was at a co-worker's Super bowl party. By the start of the fourth quarter all the good stuff was gone so we made due with rice cakes and Heineken. After one bite of the Styrofoam-quality ufo "cake" I was ready to fling it back to Mars. I suspected my actions would be frowned upon so it was a good thing I accidentally dropped it on the floor...and stepped on it.

With Coco wanting to chase something and me suddenly wanting to make up for that unflung desire, the obvious action is to give it a fling and see if she can catch it. Maybe there's a new sport in the making.

We move out into the street to get her some running room and so she does not, in her canine enthusiasm, crash into either of the kids. I figure the cake is too light to go as far as a real Frisbee, but we will see. I hold the it like a Frisbee and call to Coco "Ready, girl". Coco senses my intention and she crouches into a ready stance. I give the thing a fling and she immediately sprints after it. At about ten feet out the rice cake starts twisting and is corkscrewing for a certain crash landing. When it's a couple inches from the asphalt, Coco catches up to it and goes for the grab. She chomps down on the rice cake and it immediately cracks and crumbles into a dozen different sized pieces. Coco hits the brakes, spits out the small piece in her mouth, then goes over to sniff a couple of the bigger pieces. She trots back over to me with a "What now?" look. I shrug and head back to the garage and my book. Coco rejoins the rollerblade brigade.

With the simple background sounds of kids playing and nearby lawns getting mowed, I relax and read my paperback. Later on I hear Mrs. Woodson call out for Max and Min to come inside. I glance at my watch and see I've been reading for over an hour. It has gotten chilly and going inside sounds like a good idea to me, too. I mark my spot in the book, then wake up Jace and unhook his garage leash. He gets up and we both head for the inside door. I push the garage door button and watch as the garage door panels slowly descend and mark an end to a well spent February Sunday in Milpitas.

Rocky Run

Okay, so this morning I'm out on my Saturday morning run. It's a beautiful day and I am enjoying the spring weather. There are always some local wild life and it's fun and encouraging to see all the little critters scurrying around. I'm cruising along the last leg of my run, when I see this crow on the trail up ahead. I notice it is hopping, as crows often do, but it is hopping in the same spot, just going up and down, not hopping around, as crows are wont do. It's like the crow is jumping an invisible rope. It takes me a good 25 seconds to get near enough to the crow to see what it's doing. It just keeps jumping straight up and down. The last few seconds, when I'm close enough to it, I can see it is actually shuffling its legs back and forth with each hop, like a boxer in training! As I get right next to it, as a joke I say "Good luck, Rocky". It raises both its wings over its head while it bounces around in a circle, then it takes flight.

Now that's not the weird part. What I didn't notice until the bird took flight, was the cross-eyed gopher that had been blocked from my view by the bird-in-training. The gopher, he's a little dude, but the first thing I notice is the attitude he is projecting through his posture. His hind quarters are pressed to the ground and his front quarters are fully extended up, so he has this aggressive stance, like a low trajectory missile, albeit a furry little missile. And to go with that, he is giving me that Catholic Teacher stare down. I'm thinking "Whoa, chill dude. I'm just cruising through" Then I see he is wearing a tiny beanie and he has a towel draped over his shoulder. I can't help myself, I yell "Hey! Mickeeey. How ya doin'?"

He says "Keep it going, kid", at least that's what I heard from him. I teli ya, I ran that last leg like I was training for Apollo. It felt good. When I got back to my place, I checked the refrig and fortunately I didn't have any raw eggs so I settled for some Gatorade and a granola bar. That's the life!

Argentina

Even when his head is shaved you can't see the pea size blemish, except when he has spent a sunny day walking along the tracks. This many years later and the mark that looks like an entrance wound, just above his left ear, still has a pinkness that becomes visible only when the rest of his head has tanned. On the back of his head, just right of center and higher up than the blemish, is a three-quarter inch crescent scar with some pock marks inside the arc. There's no pinkness to these, but they are raised up and always visible. Ask him, and he'll give you a wild story about how he got the blemish, the scar and pocks all at the same time, but not from a bullet when he was down in Argentina for the CIA, as you might think. He will tell you about how he and his older brother had a big train set when they were kids. How their dad bought them a sheet of plywood to nail the train tracks, the plastic trees and little ticket booth and other scaled scenery on to. He will tell you about how he and his brother spent hours planning out the whole 4 x 8 landscape, with the track layout, including switch locations and the supply tower for the coal carrying cars. Then he will tell you about setting up the train on the track, getting the order of cars just right. The engine in front and the caboose at the end, coal cars next to the engine and freight cars after. He and his brother were in perfect agreement on everything until they went to set the caboose on the track. For some odd reason, his brother wanted to put the caboose on backwards. At least it was backwards to him. Backwards was wrong. He and his brother got into a disagreement that escalated into an argument. As they were yelling at each other about which end of the caboose is the front end, their dad comes into the garage with a "What's all this damn yelling about?" He turns towards his dad's voice so he doesn't see the caboose come flying at his head. The toughest, hardest part of a HO scale train piece is the coupling mechanism. It is constructed to endure lots of hooking and unhooking by none-too-gentle hands. Throw one of those train pieces in a nice, tight spiral, the coupling mechanism leading the way and you've launched an aerial attack. His angry, wrong brother was also the quarterback for the flag football team so when the caboose bounced off the back of the receiver's head, it first dug in a little bit, then fell to the floor as an incomplete, but hurtful pass. As the receiver went down from the blow, the left side of his head, just above his ear, briefly rested against the tip of the soldering gun left poised on the plywood, after having just melted solder over a wire connection. He will tell you all this, but as you look in his cool eyes and listen to his precise diction, you will be inclined to think Argentina is more likely.

An Almost Brilliant Idea

Earlier today I had an almost brilliant idea. I see a lot of ads for being an Uber driver. Make good money. Work just the hours you want. Have lots of strangers inside your car. Sounds kind of appealing...except for that last part. Maybe I could work on that last part to make it more appealing to me. But what would make it more appealing? Well, the other arena I see lots of ads for is the various dating sites. There's some interest in that general topic, but all the real life stories I have heard about them have helped keep me away from them. What if I could meet the right kind of woman? One down on her luck. One that hasn't had a date in years. That has possibilities. But where would I be almost guaranteed to meet these kinds of women? Why, just outside a women's correctional facility of course! So...I could be an Uber driver who camps out at the release gate of the facility. Driving the women to their new lives, getting to know them along the way (Who did you stab and how many times did you stab him? Things like that.) and I'd be making money so if I wanted to take'em out to a nice Chinese buffet I could afford it. It all sounded dang near brilliant until I realized the nearest women's correctional facility is in Chowchilla. I have nothing against Chowchilla, but that's just a bit too far to go...

Founders Hall in 1992

As Mary and I walk from the Wagon Wheel Diner to our car, we both notice the cloud front has passed over Barstow while we were having our late lunch. On this January afternoon there is a slight breeze and as I unlock the car door for Mary, I catch a faint scent of new rain.

"Rain is headed our way" I say.

"Oh boy" Mary replies as she glances at the sky and then gets into the passenger seat.

She's a car sleeper, one of those people who loves sleeping in a moving car. With lunch in her belly and the desert's daylight softened by the cloud cover, I know I'll be as good as driving alone for the remainder of our trip to Las Vegas.

As we get back on the freeway a light rain begins to fall on us. Mary reaches for her big pillow and her Padres baseball cap she keeps stationed on the backseat. The pillow is for comfort and the cap is for safety. It's a precaution to avoid the hair speed bump she once endured.

A few years before, on our first trip from our home in Oildale, California to Disneyland, before she wore a cap, Mary had her one and only serious hair mishap. Since then her travel "entourage", as she calls it, has always included at least one baseball cap and a big pillow.

On the day before the Disney trip, our Ford Taurus went into the shop for some unexpected electrical repairs so my parents graciously let us take their Cadillac.

Dad bought the caddy new in 1988 and he was meticulous about the maintenance, both mechanically and cosmetically, from the day he drove it off the lot. He took it to his cousin's shop on 24th street for all the mechanical upkeep, but dad so enjoyed keeping his caddy clean that he always took care of that part himself. I think he bought Turtle Wax and Armor All leather care by the case. His caddy always ran great and looked grand. When he said we could borrow his powerful, spacious Cadillac for our trip, I was confident we'd have an easy and stylish drive.

Dad brought his caddy over to our place the night before our trip so Mary and I could get an early start the next day. He knew the place we were renting at the time didn't have a garage, but at least we had a driveway so his car would be off the street.

As a thank-you, Mary and I treated dad and mom to pork chops, mashed potatoes and apple sauce for dinner. Later on, I drove them back to their place. On the drive I asked dad if he wanted me to clean the car before returning it to him. He said to just return it with a full tank of gas and no scratches. He'd detail it himself after we returned it to him. I guessed that would be his reply.

When we left Oildale the next day, the morning fog was mostly gone, but during the night the fog had been dense enough to leave beads of water on every hard surface it could touch, including dad's car. Even the door handles were wet. After I squeegeed the front windshield and dried most of the exterior chrome, I helped Mary into the passenger seat and we got on the road.

About half an hour into the drive, Mary grabbed the small pillow she'd put in her duffle bag and she set it between herself and the car window. She nestled against the pillow, closed her eyes and said "Wake me when we get there."

I'm not sure this is exactly how her hair mishap happened, but it is my best guess. You see, the road between Oildale and Anaheim has some twists and turns, along with some elevation changes mixed in. I suspect that while Mary was peacefully leaning against her car door, with her head on the small pillow and her petite bottom in the grand leather seat, she became a victim of inertia and the slippery leather seat.

As we were going highway speeds through a number of right hand turns, momentum pushed Mary's bottom away from the passenger door and towards the center console. With each inch she slid over, she also slide down the window. Well, I guess her head slide down the window. It happened that the inside of the window had become just a bit damp because of some fog related condensation on the inside. While Mary peacefully slept, the wet window worked against her otherwise reasonable hair. As her head slid further down the window, the dampness of the glass caused part of her hair to continue to cling to the window.

Her hair was, and still is, very beautiful. It's a light brown color, straight and plentiful, but the individual strands are thin and lightweight. When she first rested against the car door, with the pillow between her and the window, she was safe and dry. As she slid towards the center console, her head must have moved off of the pillow and come in contact with the moistened glass. The dampness on the passenger side window was able to hold her hair in place as the rest of her continued to slide further down the side window.

She'd been sleeping. I'd been driving and watching traffic. Neither of us noticed the problem until we pulled into a parking space at the Magic Kingdom. When I went to wake her I noticed some of her hair was stuck against the window, but I didn't think that much of it. I gently tell her "Sleeping Beauty, we're here. " Then I pop out of car to scan the lot for one of the courtesy shuttles I'd seen trekking about. Before I spot one, I hear Mary shriek

"My hair".

I quickly drop back down into the car and look to see what's upset her. She's looking at herself in the car visor mirror and then she turns to me. Her hair that had been stuck against the window is now coming up off the right side of her head like a cresting ocean wave. With the green turtleneck sweater she is wearing, I can't help but think "Nice Gumby look". Of course I don't say that to my wife. To Mary I say

"The wet window! It whacked your hair! Can you comb it down?"

As I ask, she is already digging through her purse. She pulls out her comb and starts attacking the hair swell. It goes down, but not completely away. Instead of the hair swell rising up from the side of her head, it is now just sticking out from her head. She's gone from a Gumby shaped head to a kind of one sided block head.

As she continues to run her brush over the troubled area, I'm not sure what to say or do. I look away, out the front window. I see a family walking towards the park entrance. The two boys are wearing baseball caps. "What about wearing a hat or a cap? That will cover it up and help get it back under control." She stops combing and looks around. She sees the other families headed towards the front entrance. "That will work." she answers.

I remember that along with my softball bat and glove, I have my Padres cap stored in the trunk of our Taurus. I automatically start to go get it but soon as I grab the car keys from the ignition I realize we are in dad's caddy. I pause for a second and then decide to check the trunk anyway.

As I suspected, the trunk is neatly organized, with small red toolbox wedged against the driver side wall. Next to it, held in place by a bungee cord, is a cardboard box with car wax, a spray bottle of window cleaner, a roll of paper towels, a fly swatter and some of the mechanic's rags. It's clean and well organized so it is immediately obvious there is no cap or hat back there.

I close the trunk and as I walk back to the driver's door, I wonder if any of the souvenir shops are open already. I look towards the entrance. I can't tell for sure but I figure I'll offer to go look while Mary tries to calm down her hair.

As I stick my head through the open driver's side window, I start to tell Mary "I'll go get you a ..." and to my surprise I see she is already sporting a dark blue cap that has NAVY in bold, gold lettering across the front. "Hey, where'd you find that?" I ask. "Under the seat. I dropped my brush and it went under the seat. When I was reaching around for it I found this hat, too. What do you think?" "Must be one of my dad's hats. Fits good, looks good. I'm sure he won't mind you wearing it" Mary smiles, flips up the visor and says "Let's go find Mickey".

We had a full day's worth of run at Disneyland. Mary wore the hat the whole time and all the way back home, too. Dad and she agreed it is her hat to keep.

We are 95 miles east of Barstow and Mary is peacefully asleep. The freeway is mostly empty now, with just a few vehicles heading west and even fewer heading towards Vegas. The clouds have merged into the early evening darkness. The rain continues to fall. The quiet rhythm of the windshield wipers and the warmness of the car heater start to wear down my concentration. I feel myself gently sinking, my head is tipping forward. I'm dangerously close to nodding off, but I catch myself just as my chin hits my chest. I startle myself back to alertness, lifting my head, sitting up straight and raising my eye brows when suddenly an all-encompassing flash of lightning blasts across the sky. It is quickly followed by a peal of thunder. That slaps me back to complete alertness. "Wow, that was close to us" I say to myself. Mary sleeps.

The fright of falling asleep at the wheel and the sudden, unexpected flash-and-boom jolt me wide awake. I shake off the weariness and refocus on the road ahead and the destination waiting for us.

That lightning was so strong and unexpected it had an effect like a surprise flash photo. There was the blinding flash and then a very brief after-image. When the lightning struck, it illuminated the entire desert around us. That is, the entire desert except for a piece just off the front passenger side of the car. As we continue towards Vegas, I revisit that flash image in my mind. I clearly see the steering wheel in my hands. In the brightness I see the dashboard lights, the hood of my car, and the road ahead of us. Most of the surrounding desert is there. The one flaw in this mental photograph is just beyond the front bumper, on the shoulder of the road. Instead of a sandy shoulder, followed by barbed wire stretched between fence posts and a continuation of the desert, I see a pitch black silhouette, an ink blot that somehow got spilled onto this otherwise vivid image. Maybe it's just a burn spot from the lightning flash itself, like one of those blacked out areas in your vision right after a camera flash goes off in your face.

Not knowing whether this inkblot was created in my mind or was an unexplained piece of reality causes a curious bone in me to itch. Since there's no traffic behind me, I decide to slow down a bit and see if another lightning strike pops out of the clouds and clears up this matter.

Before we go another 10 seconds, the agitated clouds give forth two, quick, low intensity flashes. They happen as I'm glancing in the rear-view mirror. I see the reality behind me. There is something back on the side of the road. It is difficult to say for certain, but it appears to be an old car. I don't know the old car makers or models but to me it looks like a gangster car from some old 1940s Jimmy Cagney movie. It is a black sedan with big body curves, a large front grill, and two dinner plate size headlights. The lightning flashes were quick and I was looking in the mirror, but from what I saw, the car looked to be in decent shape. The paint and grill had a shiny, just-polished look, but it could have been just the rain's reflection.

I realize even with light traffic I've slowed down too much for traveling on a highway. As I get us back up to speed, I wonder why someone would leave a classic like that out in the harsh desert elements. An American classic like that should be well maintained and well cared for. Well, maybe it broke down.

I never like to see someone have car trouble, but I have never stopped to assist anyone. There is a cautionary side of me that always defeats the philanthropic urge to help. Strangely, as I think about that abandoned car, I glance in the rear-view mirror one more time and the thought of pulling over and offering to help the owner doesn't seem so outrageous.

A lot of the drive between Barstow and Las Vegas is long low inclines followed by long low declines. For the next few minutes we climb one of those inclines. People may think the desert is completely flat, but it's not. Those 140 miles before Vegas are a continuous series of modest elevation changes. It's more like traveling over a bunch of nearly flattened 'M's rather than just a flat line.

We drive on. The rain has nearly stopped, but the lightning and thunder still want to have their fun. Mary peacefully sleeps through all the desert's evening serenade. As we start the next ascent there are two more flashes of lightning, but not so near the highway. They and their friends are moving off to the southwest, but as they go their

34

way they reveal an augur of the night. After seeing the silhouette of the car and taking on the curiosity of its predicament, I have been absorbing and processing what each flash exposes. In this case, the first of these flashes reveals the outline of a man. As I ponder the unlikelihood of such an occurrence, the second flash confirms my sighting. A man stands on the shoulder of the road, about 80 yards in front of my slowing car.

As the car lights bring him into view, he throws down his cigarette, stamps it out and starts to unbutton his overcoat. He watches us approach. Naturally, I pull the car to a stop right in front of him and silently watch as he finishes removing his overcoat, folds it over his forearm, removes his hat and calmly climbs into the back seat of my car. What the hell am I doing? Moreover, what the heck will Mary think ?

He sets his hat on top of his coat he's already laid on the seat next to him. His movements show a confidence and when he looks at me I see it in his demeanor, too. As our eyes lock, he reaches forward to shake my hand. His hand is warmer than mine. "Thanks" he says, then he lets go of my hand and relaxes against the back of the seat. I nod and turn around to drive, as if I do this type of thing for a living.

He is average height and build, but very well dressed. Besides the overcoat and the fedora, he wears a gray herringbone jacket, black slacks with neatly pressed creases, a glossy white shirt and a simple, thin black tie. His face looks a bit pale, but considering he had been standing in the desert night, that is much less a surprise than his warm hand.

Once we are back on the road and up to speed, my cautious nature makes a comeback. I look in the rear view mirror at him. He sees my wary glance and gives back a smile.

"I'm Benjamin. I appreciate the lift" he says.

"I'm Clive and sleeping beauty here is my wife, Mary. We're heading to Las Vegas... Staying at the Flamingo" I add.

He leans forward a bit and smiles. "Oh yeah? Why the Flamingo?" he asks, with a touch of happiness in his voice.

I tell him we like old school Vegas and the Flamingo is one of the few original casinos still in play. "I think it was built in the '40s. Some of the original Flamingo hotel is still there." He takes it in with a relaxed nod. Turns out he knows a lot about the older hotels and casinos. A warmness comes to his face as he talks.

"Did you know Jimmy Durante was the headliner when the Flamingo opened in December of '46? Took some convincing to pry him away from his Hollywood lifestyle, but he loved the Flamingo and put on a great show."

I tell him "I read online that the opening was considered a flop. Some freak rainstorm, sort of like tonight's, but more serious, kept lots of the Flamingo's invited guests stuck in LA."

"Did the writer of that article talk to anyone who was actually at the opening?" Benjamin asks.

"No, not that I recall." I reply.

"Too bad. He might have gotten it right if he did his homework."

Benjamin continues "The Flamingo was the third big casino to open in Vegas. El Rancho and Frontier were there first, but when the Flamingo opened it was classy, not like those sawdust cowboy joints. The Flamingo was class, top to bottom. The entertainment was top notch. The games were on the up and up. The staff always wore tuxedos. "

I jump in with "What really impressed me on our first visit was the pool. There's no other pool with the scalloped edge and a fountain in the center. It somehow goes with the flamingo motif". Benjamin smiles and says "Yeah, I like it, too." "In Viva Las Vegas, Elvis and Ann Margret have a scene where he falls into the pool from a high dive."

Benjamin and I continue to talk all the way to the Flamingo entrance. As we pull to a stop under the huge, brightly lit awning of the Flamingo, Benjamin quietly opens his car door. Mary slept through all our yapping on the drive, but with the car in park, she wakes up, does her stretch and growl routine, then asks "Are we there, yet?" While I start to answer her, I hear the car door close. Mary looks around, sees the neon lights and knows we've arrived. I want to try to slow down Ben before he can disappear into the casino. I pop out of the car and call to him "Ben, Ben, hold up. Will we see you inside?" I know he hears me, but he keeps walking towards the glass doors. Without stopping, he looks back towards us and says

"Bet your room and I guarantee it."

I hear him clearly, but I don't understand.

"What?" I think. "Bet the room ? What can that mean?" I ask myself.

"Welcome to the Flamingo" says the valet attendant.

I hear Mary getting out of the car and I watch Benjamin pass through the hotel doors and fade into the darkness of the casino. I'm sorry to see him go so quickly, but I'm not going to leave Mary to chase after him. I exchange my car keys for a claim slip, sling our travel bag over my shoulder and go grab Mary's hand.

As we wait to check in, Mary asks me who I was yelling at back there. "It was Benjamin." I don't tell her we picked him up out in the desert. I don't tell her he was in the backseat of our car. I don't tell her what he said as he walked away. "He likes Vegas, old Vegas, like we do." It's our turn to check in so we step up to the counter.

The previous year we accidentally got a room in the old, two story part of the Flamingo, rather than the newer high-rise. We liked the style and décor, as well as the proximity to the pool. This year we requested to stay there again. We got room 207, just one room over from the one we had last time.

We relax in our room for a while, then head to dinner and some gambling afterwards. The availability of breakfast 24 hours a day is a true indicator of a quality restaurant, in my opinion. The Flamingo coffee shop is just such an establishment. It's 7:24PM and I just ordered Eggs Benedict. Mary asked for a club sandwich and fries. It's good food and reasonable priced and the portions are not ridiculously big.

We take our time eating, then take a walk on the Strip. We cross the Strip and stroll past Caesars. I can't see the Caesars fountains without my mind playing the slow motion crash of Evel's daring fountain jump. His approach and the actual jump always quickly flash before my eyes, but as soon as the landing jars his hands off the handlebars, the scene slows down to a fifth of normal speed. His helmeted head leads his body over the front of his motorcycle. He puts out his hands to brace himself, but it does no good as he is going too fast. When he hits the pavement, his body moves like a disjointed mannequin inside a jumpsuit, bouncing and twisting and rolling over and over in awkward ways. He and his bike seem to be in a bad-tumbling competition that goes far too long. As a kid, I'd heard my dad use the expression "He fell ass over tea kettle" and I never fully understood what he meant until I saw Evel's disastrous fall. Since then I always hear dad's voice at the end crash scene. I guess putting those two things together made them both stick with me longer than either would have by itself.

After the scene has played out in my mind, Mary and I agree we got enough evening exercise so we head back to the Flamingo casino.

We both like roulette. If you play it right, it's not too expensive to play for a couple hours. We find a table with a reasonable minimum limit and each get $50 worth of chips. I have my favorite numbers, mostly based on sports figures I like. I always play thirty two, Magic, and thirty three, Bird and then I'll pick a couple combo bets. Mary plays birthdates and our wedding date, 9-17. We play for a while and neither of us hits our numbers straight up, but a couple combo bets have paid off. Still, our money is running away faster than I'd like it to.

Next to most every roulette wheel is a digital display that shows the last 20 winning numbers of that wheel. As we wait for the next spin of the wheel Mary says somewhat absentmindedly

"The last two numbers are 20 and 7, that's almost our room number."

As I check the display, the departing words of Benjamin come back to me. "Bet the room and I guarantee it." I'm still not sure what that means, but besides putting a dollar on 32 and 33, I place a dollar on 20 and a dollar on 7. Mary notices my last minute bets.

"Got a hunch?" she asks.

"I'm not sure." I reply.

The wheel is spinning, and the dealer shoots the ball around the edge. It navigates around the perimeter and then falls toward the turning wheel. My heart starts to race a bit more than usual as I wonder what Benjamin's words could mean. I know it is silly to think they mean anything.

The ball bounces in the crazy, random way it always does and then it lands with authority in the 20 slot. The wheel continues to spin, but the ball is planted on 20. The dealer calls 20 as the winner.

That's $35 to us and I'm immediately excited and afraid of betting the 7. I know I have to do it, but how much do I believe, how much do I put on the 7? Hitting the 20 is "found money", but putting all $35 on the 7 is too big, too bold for me. As I move a stack of 20 one dollar chips onto 7 straight up, Mary gives me a look of shock. She doesn't know "Bet the room".

"A bigger hunch, I see" she says.

I inhale and nod. The stack of 20 chips towers over the other bets on table.

Before the next spin, the dealer looks over at the pit boss. As we continue to place our other bets, the pit boss wonders over. He stands behind the dealer. The dealer picks the ball out of the 20 slot and shoots it into motion once again. I watch that little white ball go, hoping it is my friend a second time in a row. Mary reaches over and squeezes my slightly sweaty hand. The ball starts its descent to a decision. I know it is not going to be work. Twenty, seven, twenty just happened and that is the end of it. There is no magic, just a bit of coincidence.

The ball finally falls into the spinning wheel. It hops and bops around, on one number and then another. I spot the 7 and decide to follow it around the wheel, rather than track the ball. Just as the seven is nearest to Mary and me, that beautiful, wonderful, truly magical white ball lands in the perfect slot, 7.

That lifts me out of my seat. I let out a "Yes", accented with a fist pump. Mary has her hand up for a high five. I clap her hand and give her a quick kiss.

"How much is that?" I ask.

I don't know why I hadn't done the math when placing the bet, but I am quickly working on it. Twenty dollars times the 35-to-1 payout is...

"Seven hundred" Mary says as she points towards the dealer. As the dealer slides over 100 roulette chips with 6 black $100 chips on top of the stack, she says

"That's 700, sir. Congratulation. Nicely done".

Icing on a cake never looked as good as those 6 black chips topping the roulette tokens.

I toss the dealer a couple roulette chips as a tip and exchange a $100 chip for 4 twenty five dollar chips. Now I am a believer. "The room, one more time." I say as I put $50 on 20. The pit boss hovers as the dealer does her thing again. The wheel spins and she shoots the ball in the opposite direction. The ball does its first couple laps up at the perimeter and then falls towards the numbers. Mary squeezes my hand like she is in labor. The first number the ball hits is the 20 but the wheel is spinning too fast and kicks the ball out. The next number for the ball is the 7, but the wheel is still just a little too fast. Mary and I both watch the 20 slot and wait for the ball to get back to it. The ball tap dances with a couple other numbers and comes to rest on 35.

Thirty five? It is supposed to be 20 and 7 forever ! I hit 20 once and then 7 once (207 once) and that's it? Seeing the first 20-7 brought out a hunch, then with hitting that 20, in a flash I became a believer in "Bet the room", and now I know the flash is gone. Whatever was in that flash, that brief good-luck thunderstorm, has moved on. We stay for two more spins to make sure. Thirty five is followed by double zero and eleven.

"I'm ready to cash out." I tell Mary.

She agrees. We cash out with a combined $685 in chips. I know that holding that cash will be a wonderful, uplifting, and enlivening feeling. Mary and I are what folks would call teetotalers. We rarely drink alcohol, even when sitting at the roulette table. However, we both are big ice cream and gelato fanatics. Our winnings have triggered the desire for a celebration. We both have the urge for a well appointed cup or cone of ice cream. As we trade in the chips for folding money, I ask the cashier if there's an ice cream parlor in the hotel. He says "It's just past the jewelry shop on Founder's Hall" and points us in the right direction. We float that way.

Although the jewelry shop doesn't have any Rocky Road or Mint Chip, as we walk by it, Mary's appetite directs her towards some of the candy on display there. We stop so Mary can ogle what's on display in the windows. As we look over the diamonds and emeralds, someone walks up behind us. I don't hear him approach but I sense him there, then I feel a hand light on my shoulder. I turn and look right behind me. Oddly, no one is there. I look down the hall, towards the ice cream parlor and no one is there, either.

As I am turning back to look at the earrings Mary is talking about, I see something that blanches me. Mary sees my paleness and thinks it is caused by the price tag on the earrings she is interested in.

"Two fifty is not that bad. Don't faint." she says somewhat jokingly.

In a halting voice I reply "Oh no... it's not that much."

"But you look so pale, I thought you were going to" I jump in with "I'm fine." But I'm not. What I had just seen, what had caught my eye, was a transparent reflection of Benjamin right there. Imposed on the glass of the jewelry shop was a crisp, clean image of him, leaning forward just a bit, smiling, like he was about to offer me a warm handshake. He's in that same sharp suit he was wearing earlier.

Mary's pointing at another earring set and I'm looking towards it. I'm half listening to her as she talks about birth stones and not liking dangling earrings and such, all the while I ruminate over how I could have seen Benjamin, without him being there.

I'm not prone to seeing things that are not there so I take stock of what's happened. I just felt someone behind me, but no one was there. I just saw a reflection of someone, but he disappeared. What's going on? I have to look down the hall a second time. Still no one is there, but rather than turn back to the jewelry shop, I turn towards the opposite side of the hallway. Across the hall, along the other wall, is a set of portrait photographs. Off to the side of where we were standing is a portrait of a man that looks very much like Benjamin. I have to get a closer look at the photo so I walk over to it. Under the photo it says "Benjamin Seigel, founder of the Flamingo Hotel and Casino". My brain slows down as I cautiously put together some strange pieces from the day. During a desert rainstorm, lightning revealed a well maintained "gangster" car. In that same rainstorm, a man named Benjamin waited on the shoulder of the road for me to pick him up. For over 30 minutes he talked about the Vegas he knows and loves, old Vegas. That Benjamin, today's Benjamin, is looking at me from a photo taken over 48 years ago. I remember reading that Benjamin Seigel, reputed gangster and the Flamingo's founder, was assassinated in Los Angeles in 1945.

That bone of curiosity I felt earlier in the night has suddenly grown into a full skeleton of eeriness and wonderment. Everyone knows Las Vegas is the land of possibilities. It is full of magicians, hypnotists and impersonators, but I have never heard of a Benjamin Seigel impersonator. Today's Benjamin was articulate, cultured and 100% real. We talked, he knew Vegas things I didn't know. Yet he practically vanished just as he made a unique and difficult guarantee, a guarantee that traveled beyond coincidence and went all the way to an unlikely winning resolution in a city where the wheel usually spins for the casino. I now stand in front of him and see he kept his word. I had asked Benjamin "Will we see you inside?" and he replied "Bet the room and I guarantee it".

I stand glued to the carpet in front of Benjamin's photo, trying to visually drill into the picture for an answer. I inspect his jacket, his shirt and tie, his face and how his hair is combed. I look at his hands and how they are folded in front of him. I'm searching for some flaw, some clue, that will lead to an explanation. I look into Benjamin's eyes and murmur "Will I see you again, Benjamin?" It looks as if he knows, but he isn't going to talk right now.

Mary announces that it looks like the ice cream parlor may be closing and we better get a move on. I just notice she has come up beside me and taken my hand. She pulls my focus back into comfortable reality and as we head down the hall I think about how much I like old Vegas, particularly the mysterious Flamingo. Thanks, Benjamin.

The Russian Motorcyclist

Earlier this week I was driving home from work. Part of my drive is on the 101 freeway. I was in the right lane cruising along at a mere 68 miles per hour when I noticed a motorcyclist approaching me in the left lane. I was a motorcyclist in my past so I give them a little more attention than I would otherwise. As the guy gets closer, I get this feeling he is Russian. I don't know why, it's not like he has a Stalin mustache or a Putin scowl. The thought just pops into my head. Since I'm driving I have to check traffic around me, I can't just watch this guy get closer. After I check my surroundings I glance in my mirror again and he is gone. Oh, he's already right beside me. Like I said, I've ridden motorcycles for over 20 years so I'm curious. I look over to my left at what he is riding. It's a Triumph. Not an old one, but a fairly new one. I can tell this because how clean the cycle is. What I also notice is the guy has a dog with him. I'm not talking about in a basket behind him or in a crate in front of him, no! This motorcycle guy, going 70+ on the freeway, has a dog on his lap. I quickly look to see if the dog has a harness holding him to his master. No. Is there some foot holds on the tank for the dog. No. The dog is riding buck naked and paws free. A dog on his lap. Imagine that. It'd be like balancing a watermelon on your lap as you book down the road. As far as I can tell, the dog's front paws are simply resting on the slippery surface of the gas tank. Wa-oh-nelly. That seems pretty darn dog scary to me so I glance at the dog's face to see if it is freaking out or anything. That's when things get weird. The dog seems calm, but for the very first time I notice there is a squirrel riding piggy back on the dog. I'm kind of shocked by this revelation. Vladmir is driving. His dog is on the tank, and there's a squirrel hanging onto the dog. The dog's squirrel, not surprisingly, wearing a leather skull cap and googles, has its hind legs wrapped around the dog's neck and with its front paws it is hold on to dog's ears like they are handle bars. Oh, and on top of the squirrel is a mouse in an Uncle Sam outfit. I know. Things just keep getting smaller and smaller. This patriotic mouse is fascinating me. Way back, 5 seconds ago I thought "Wow, a dog on a motorcycle is odd". Then I saw the squirrel and I thought "How bizarre!!" Now I see the red, white and blue decorated mouse and I think "I wouldn't be a bit surprised if that mouse was holding aloft a tiny statue of liberty like it was charging into battle, with Lady Liberty as its sword of justice." And don't you know that's exactly what it was doing. There's a brief pause and then they all turn to me, the mouse, the squirrel, the dog and Vladmir, and with the wind whipping through their hair/fur/coat they all give me a big smile. It's a pyramid of happiness and in that moment I'm loving all that is good with America. They cruise on up ahead of me and I get back to some Joe Satriana music and my own open road.

June Bugs

Summertime for a youngster in the San Joaquin Valley of California means living in shorts or swim trunks, having blistered, then calloused bare feet, finding afternoon shade, or better yet, a friend with a pool. It means waking up with the swamp cooler already going and staying off the blacktop, even an hour after the sun has set. It also means June bugs.

The June bug is an interesting insect to both young and old. Only seen at night and only around the month of June, they are a known but eerie icon of overwarmed summer evenings. To say the San Joaquin June bug can be larger than a bubble bee is true, but to say it is as big as a walnut would be an exaggeration. There are two sizes of June bugs here and both fit within these size limits. The smaller June bug has a shell that is almost the brownish color of peanut skin, but with an orange tint to it. The larger June bug has a darker grayish green color, as if it was painted a forest green and then dusted with charcoal ash. The larger ones also have two prominent antennas and a prehensile tail. Okay, I made up the bit about having a prehensile tail, but the two antennas are real.

Not everyone remembers the very first time a June bug buzzed into their lives, but everyone that has sweltered a summer somewhere between Bakersfield and Sacramento has a June bug story. One of my favorites is actually my younger brother's story.

Back when our dad worked out of town during the week, he'd get home on Friday night and it was always a competition for his time. Sometimes he'd go play poker with his brothers and his dad. Sometimes Nancy would come over and babysit us while he and mom would run off to the movies. Sometimes Jake and I would get to go fishing with him.

On the last Friday in June it was our turn. We loaded up the rods and reels, the tackle box, the frozen anchovies, lawn chairs and the propane lantern, and then headed for the California aqueduct. We got there a bit before dusk and found a spot on the canal bank. The standard operating procedure for Jake and me was to get our lines in the canal as quick as possible, then go talk with all the other fishermen to see what they were catching and what bait they were using, and so on. Dad would watch our poles while we were gone.

For me, it was always about seeing the caught fish in people's buckets or on their stringers. Striper and catfish were the most common catches on the aqueduct, and we saw a few of each most times we went out. It was still odd and interesting to me to see them since they didn't exist anywhere else, not at Tubby's Pet Shop, nor in the little trout-stocked pond we sometimes fished on Saturday mornings.

For Jake it was about the fish, but it was more about the people and talking with them. I'd look in their fish buckets or ask them if they'd caught anything. Jake would ask them how they were doing, how long they'd been there, had they missed any strikes or had one get away. He knew how to talk with people.

On this Friday, after baiting hooks with chunks of anchovy, clipping on 2 ounce weights, casting and setting the lines, we started on our rounds. There were around a dozen groups of fishermen spread out amongst the two canal banks and the concrete bridge that spanned the banks.

The first two groups were getting setup so we just said a quick 'hi' as we walked on. Next was an elderly lady that we always saw there. Most folks brought a lawn chair or a stool to sit on. Most folks brought a plastic bucket to hold their fish. She never had neither. She sat herself right on the gravelly bank and to hold the fish she caught she used a stringer on the end of a rope. She fished with a stiff pole dad said was a deep sea rig. Sometimes she holds on to her pole and sometimes, like this time, she has it in the rod holder that she's pushed into the ground.

As we walk up to her, I see she is just putting her rosary beads into the big pocket of her fishing vest. She turns to us and says

"Hello, boys. Did ya just get here?"

"Yes, maam." we answer

I notice there's a rope traveling from the rod holder, along the bank and then down the 10 feet of the dry, sloped, canal bank. It disappears into the water.

Looking at the rope, I ask "Anything so far Mrs. Tano?"

Jake jumps in with "Yea, Mrs. Tano, what'd ya have on the stringer?"

Mrs. Tano glances down to where her stringer disappears into the aqueduct's dark water and says

"Haul it up and take a look."

Since I'm closest to the rope, I grab it and start pulling it up and out of the water. As I get a second handful of rope, I turn to Jake and say expectantly "Feels like something." Jake's looking at were the stringer is starting to come up out of the water. Mrs. Tano has already turned back to her fishing but I see she has cracked a small smile and gives a nod to my comment.

There's no confusing a striper with a catfish. Stripers are silvery, sleek and shiny sided, with a shape somewhat akin to a football. Catfish are mud colored on top and a dull, dirty white on the bottom side. They have the shape of the meaty end of baseball bat. As soon as I saw the head emerge from the water I knew it was a striper on the stringer.

Still watching the tip of her pole, Mrs. Tano informs us "Caught him about 20 minutes ago."

"That's a big one. What'd you use for bait? Did he put up a good fight? What'd think he weighs?" Jake fires off.

"Bait was Anchovy head. With this rig, I brought him in nice and easy. No fussin' and no fightin'. I weighed him in at a tad under 6 pounds." She turns to me and says "Ease him back into the water, son." I let the rope slide out of my hands and watch the fish sink back into the canal.

With that, Mrs. Tano reaches into another vest pocket, pulls out a cigarette and puts it in the side of her mouth. She finds a stick match in the same pocket, lights it off a strike patch she's sewn onto the pocket flap and puts the flame to her smoke. After a draw, she gives us another smile and says "You boys better scoot on and finish your visitin' before it gets too dark."

At one end of the aqueduct's fishing area is the road that we take to get here. At the other end of the fishing area is an oversized concrete foot bridge connecting the two sides of the canal. The bridge is wide enough that people can fish right opposite of each other, one casting upstream and one casting downstream, without too much worry of hooking the other person when making a cast. This also gives Jake and me plenty of room to walk along on our trek. The odd, eerie thing about this bridge is that the side walls are about 6 feet tall and solid cement. Neither of us is tall enough to see over the wall and when the sun is nearly done for the day, there's a cave-like feeling down there. Because the walls are so tall, everyone that fishes from the bridge brings some type of platform to stand on. Wooden benches from picnic tables are the most popular item, second most common is two plastic buckets with boards between them.

It's quieter and darker down in the foot bridge and the adults on their fishing platforms loom much larger over us. We always keep close together and just glance in people's fishing buckets as we hunker down and get over to the other side of the canal.

The first bucket we see has a small June bug walking the rim and a two pound catfish curled up in the water. The man fishing doesn't notice us.

The next man is not fishing, but it is clear he is getting ready to because he's chopping bait. It looks like he has a few anchovies laid out head to tail on his picnic bench and he is chunking them up with a butcher knife. Jake and I have never seen any of those slasher movies where some fiend uses just such a knife to cause mayhem, but we still have a wariness about us as we approach him.

He notices us just as his arm reaches its peak. With his arm paused high above his head, he turns towards us. "Hello boys" he says as his arm falls from the sky and the knife cleaves off another inch of bait. He sets the knife on the bench and picks up the first three pieces of bait. He extends his hand with the bait towards us and with an expectant smile on his face he asks "You boys fishing tonight? Need any bait?"

I've never seen green anchovies, but that seems to be what he is offering us. A fisherman is always willing to try different baits, different hook setups and lures, so we move in for a closer look. The man politely moves his hand closer to us, too. Jake comments

"That's weird looking anchovy."

"Is it?" the man says.

I stare at the chunks in his hand. It takes me one blink to realize he's not holding bait fish in his hand. It takes me another blink to realize the 3 pieces in his hand are the head and body pieces of a small Garter snake.

"That's a snake head" Jake whispers as he stands perfectly still.

The man is close enough to hear Jake.

"Take it, it's the best part" he says.

I look from the man's hand to his face. In the darkening twilight his eyes have taken on a cataract glassiness like our neighbor's old Labrador dog. Whether it is the politeness I'd been taught, the shock of snake parts or his glassy eyes, I feel stuck in place and with nothing else to do, my right hand starts to move toward his offerings.

My arm movement must have unstuck Jake, cause I feel him tug on my shirt sleeve and say "Bill, let's get going." That snaps it for me and the man, too. I pull my hand back and he blinks away the glassiness. Jake bumps me into motion.

After that we make quick work of the rest of the bridge. No talking and just glancing into buckets and fish pails. We quickly get off the bridge and turn towards the folks fishing the opposite side of the canal from our spot. There are only a few groups.

We skip the teenage couple, giggling and squirming around with each other on a blanket. Their fishing poles are just laying flat on the ground and no lines in the water.

The next group is a father and his son. We know Tommy Jr, "TJ", from school. He was in Jake's class last year and may be in his class again this coming school year since there are only 2 fifth grade teachers at our school. TJ's dad is in his lawn chair, with his can of soda in the holder and the latest Reader's Digest opened up in front of him. His line is already in the aqueduct. TJ is just winding up to make his cast.

"Hey, TJ" Jake says as Tommy pauses at the end of his back swing.

Tommy looks over to us. "Hey Jake. Hey Bill." he says and then starts his cast. Fishing on the aqueduct does not take fine tuned casting skills. The aqueduct is a long, wide, unchanging, unchallenging trough of water. Cast as you like, but we cast for the unreachable far side, the opposite bank of the canal. Casting here is about distance and hang time.

We all watch TJ's tackle sail out over the water. We all listen to the line quickly, quietly play out of his reel. In those few seconds that the tackle is flying across the sky, there's a kind of innocent desire, a secret impossible hope that the sinker, the baited hooks, the whole shebang, will just keep flying upward. The line will not give in to earth's gravity, but will keep ascending, like a rocket to Mars. The line will play out all the way until our grip is tested, until we are pulled up, flying across the sky towards a land of some great Buck Rodgers adventure.

TJ poses with his casting arm extended out and up, his fishing pole pointing towards a distance galaxy, ready to go if he is so lucky.

We see and hear his tackle splash down somewhere near the halfway point of the aqueduct. After TJ sets his line and puts his pole in the holder, Jake asks what bait they are using.

"Worms, big old night crawlers" TJ replies.

"Trying for catfish tonight ?" Jake asks.

"Yep, and dad already got a bite."

Mr. Rakes looks up from his Digest and gives us a friendly

"Hey, boys. Your dad still working out of town ?"

"Hi Mr. Rakes. He got home tonight. We just got setup on the other side" I say.

Mr. Rakes looks across the way. He sees our dad, then nods and turns to us. "Tell him I say 'hi'"

"Sure thing, Mr. Rakes" I reply.

We talk with TJ for a while about how the Dodgers and the Angels are doing, about school starting in a few weeks, who is the meanest teacher, and who is the nicest teacher. Talk slows down. Jake and I notice it is getting dark enough to light the lantern so we race back to our spot, ignoring the last group of fisherman and then using the road to cross back to our side of the canal. If we don't get back in time, dad will light the lantern himself and there's no fun in that.

Dad looks towards us as we race up to him. That triggers both Jake and me to simultaneously ask

"Can I light the lantern, dad ?" followed by "No, me, dad. It's my turn!" By the time he pulls the matchbox from his pocket, we are standing before him, eagerly awaiting his decision.

He bends down and sets the matchbox on the lantern cap. When he stands up he pronounces to us "Rock, paper, scissors".

"Two out of three?" Jake asks me.

"Yesss, it's always two out of three" I reply.

Three throws of rock, paper, scissors and I win. Jake still hasn't realized that his third throw is always paper.

While I'm trying to light the lantern, Jake wonders off a bit and, to deal with losing, he starts picking up small rocks and chucking them into the aqueduct. I strike the match to life and put the flame into the lantern's clear cylinder. Then I turn open the propane feed. There's just a quick second of hissing before the wick lights up. I pull out the dead match and reduce the propane feed until dad tells me "That's good".

With that done, I look to see if Jake is still throwing rocks. I see he's bending down to pick one up, but he's looking at the lantern as he reaches. He doesn't notice that rather than a rock, he's grabbed a large June bug. I get as far as opening my mouth to tell him this, when he quickly throws the bug towards the aqueduct. Of course June bugs can fly, why this one didn't is why this story exists. The June bug sailed out over the water without any attempt to fly, then it splashed down in the aqueduct's southern-California bound current. It was a quieter splash than what Jake's rocks had made, not even audible. The aqueduct current is consistent and strong, the June bug starts to float towards Los Angeles but only gets a few feet before something comes up through the water' surface and engulfs it. A big open maw, a flash of silver, the slap of a tail fin against the surface, then calm again.

I see all of this and a "wooh" escapes me. Jake asks "What was that?"

"Some gigantic striper just ate the June bug you threw" I explain.

"I didn't throw any June bug" he protests.

"You did. You weren't looking at what you picked up. It was a June bug".

After a pause, Jake asks "Dad, will a striper hit a June bug?"

"It might" dad replies.

Jake steps up to his rod, lifts it out of the holder and begins to reel it in. He gets the line all the way in. Dad must know what Jake has in mind because he tells Jake to not chuck the bait he's been using. "Just set your bait with the rest of the anchovies, son."

Jake takes the bait off the hook and sets it on the paper plate with the other chunks already cut up. Then he starts inspecting the ground.

After a minute he says "Bill, help me find a June bug."

"Even if you find one, how you gonna fish with it?"

"I'll just … hook it through the belly." Jake replies

"But it won't even float. It'll sink cause of the weight." I argue.

Jakes keeps scanning the ground around the lantern, then he stops to think. "I'll use a small weight at the end of line, and a bobber right next to the weight to keep it from sinking...and a hook on a leader, up from the bobber."

We both turn to dad. With a nod, he says "Give it a shot."

Now we are both searching the ground around the lantern. Nothing at first, then I see one. "Jake, there's one climbing on this side of the lantern".

"Grab it, Bill" he says as he moves to change his setup. June bugs are as harmless as Lady Bugs. A June bug will crawl on your arm, your chest, or across your baseball cap, without so much as a care. I didn't grab this one so much as I let it crawl into the palm of my hand.

By the time I had it, Jake had pulled a bobber from the tackle box and was hooking it on to the same swivel that held the small weight. I let the bug hike up towards my elbow, while Jake looped the leader through the slipknot he'd put six inches up from the weight. He snugged up the slipknot and then pinched the hook between the thumb and index finger of his right hand. Without a word, he reaches over with his left hand and pulls the June bug off my forearm. With a focus and skill he usually saves for a keepsies game of marbles, Jake carefully threads the hook through the June bug. In one smooth motion he runs the hook from the front underside of the body, through the torso and out the back underside. Just the barbed tip is sticking out between the last pair of legs.

Jake lets go of the June bug and hook. He picks up the pole. Dad and I can see the June bug's legs are still working, even with the hook through its body. As Jake takes the rod back for his cast, dad gets up and moves over close to him. Dad tells Jake to cast smoothly, so as to not cause the bug to get thrown off, and to aim a bit upstream to give it more float time. Jake looks out towards where he has been throwing his disappointment and then he angles his rod upstream from that.

Jake casts. All three of us watch as the weight, bobber and bug fly up and away from us. With the line connecting all of them back to Jake, they start to descend. They splash down about ten feet north of where the monster appeared. Jake sets the line and watches as the rig starts to drift with the current.

"Keep an eye on your line, son. If it gets too much slack, reel some of it in." dad tells him.

I can see the red and white bobber, but it has gotten dark enough that I cannot see if the June bug is floating along or not. The bobber passes the spot of attack and I tell Jake

"The bobber just passed the spot."

"Good." Jake says, "Then my bug is about there."

I look even closer at the bobber, then upstream from it. Now I can see the June bug is, indeed, floating a tad upstream from the red and white buoy.

"I see it !" I say. Jake quickly looks over at me and asks "The fish?" I turn to him and reply "No, no, the June bug".

"Ohh..." he replies.

Before Jake or I have turned back to watch his line, we hear a splash. I jump my eyes back to where I last saw the bobber and June bug. Both are out of sight. I hear Jake gasp. I look over and see him, through clenched jaw saying something that sounds like "nooo you doon't" . His fishing pole is quivering in his hands. The line has drawn tight and the tip of the rod is bent and jittery. Jake has tightened up, too. He's squeezed his elbows in against his body and his shoulders are pinched up nearly to his ears. With his left hand he's got a tight grip on the pole, but with his right hand he's fumbling to work the reel. At first, he can't find the handle, and when he does, he can't remember which way to crank it. I'm thinking the fish might spit the bait and get away.

"Jake, set the hook" dad says in a calm voice. Dad's voice and advice help. Jake gives the rod a quick pull and sets the hook. He finds the handle and starts to work it the right way.

Jake has caught plenty of fish. He's landed bluegill, crappy, and a few planted trout. The weekend we camped at Bass Lake, he caught a tasty 14 inch big mouth bass we had for dinner that night. Here at the aqueduct one day he brought in two catfish, or maybe the same catfish twice, but he's never landed a striper. This could be his first striper, and by the bend in the pole, it could be his biggest fish.

The fish must feel the hook now because it decides it is time to really fight. The reel's drag is set too loose to restrain the beast. The high pitched whirring sound of line being pulled out of the reel is impressive. Jake's fish is swimming away, quickly taking out more and more line. Jake reacts by cranking faster, but it's not doing any good. He even starts to back away from aqueduct's edge, as if that will help bring in the fish. Dad and I are standing on either side of him. Dad has advice again. "The reel has plenty of line, son. Just keep the pressure on. It will tire out."

All the fish Jake and I have caught were usually easy to bring in once they were hooked. They would put up a fight, but it felt more like a gentle resistance than a real battle. This one is different.

It's hard to say how long that initial run lasted. With the fish swimming away from Jake, easily defeating the drag setting, it may have been minutes. Dad and I keep scanning the dark water's surface for a hint of where the fish might break out, while Jake continues to crank on the reel. After a bit, we hear the whirring start to die down. Jake must know he is finally making progress because we hear him say "Come on, now."

The fish took lots of line out at the start of the fight but now it's giving it back. Jake is winning the tug of war. He cranks away for a while. With a little bit of panic in his voice, Jake asks "Where is it ? I can't see it."

"It's there, son. Just keep the pressure on." dad tells him.

"Keep cranking, Jake" I add.

The fish is no longer pulling out line, but it has enough strength to resist a straight reel in. Jake's poll is still bent, but it no longer quivers from the fish's energy.

We don't see the fish until Jake has it right at the water's edge.

"Dad, it's a striper!" Jake shouts. Even as Jake reels it out of the water, it flops and fights the pull of the line. And it's big, definitely Jake's biggest fish, but he still needs to get it up the 10 feet of bank, from the aqueduct's water line to the top, where we stand.

We've been at the aqueduct enough times to have seen people hook some nice size fish, only to lose their near-catch on this last section, where the fish has to be dragged up that incline.

The concrete walls of the aqueduct are angled too steep to walk on, even with their rough finish. Standing on the top of the aqueduct and pulling the fish up this rough, dry section is the only choice for us fishermen, but it adds more tension on the line if you do it wrong, if you drag the fish up the concrete. Some of the fish, as they are pulled over the rough surface, must sense this is their last chance to get away. Sometimes they struggle one last time and manage to free themselves, then flop back to freedom.

Dad tells Jake to lift the tip of his rod up high and to keep the fish's body up off the concrete as much as possible.

He follows dad's advice and lifts the rod tip while continuing to bring in the fish. All but the tail of the fish is lifted off the sloped embankment. The fish struggles, but is much weaker and Jake gets it all the way up to the top edge. Jake takes two steps backward while swinging his pole and the fish over to Jake's left. The striper is now on level ground, a good couple feet from the edge and a possible escape. Jake quickly sets down his pole and kneels down right next to his striper. He pets his fish twice and says "I got you. I got you." The fish raises its tailfin and the slowly lowers it. Without taking his eyes off of striper, he asks, "How much do you think he weighs?"

In all the excitement and concentration, none of us noticed that Mrs. Tano is with us until she speaks up. "I got my spring scale right here with me, Jake. Unhook him and we'll take a measure."

The hook is set in the corner of the striper's mouth. Not surprisingly, the bait is gone from the hook. Jake pets his fish one more time, then uses his foot to hold it still while he removes the hook. Mrs. Tano silently hands him the scale. He uses the scale's clip to pinch the striper's lip, then he stands and lifts the scale, bringing the fish up, too. We all peer at the markings on the scale, looking for the red arrow that will tell us the weight.

"Wow, seven pounds, 10 ounces! Dad, that's got to be my record!" Jake exclaims and then looks up to dad. Dad replies

"That may even be a family record. Nice going son".

We all pause and look at the fish hanging from the scale. Then Mrs. Tano says "Bill, maybe there's another one out there."

I'd forgotten about my rig. It is still cast out. I decide it's a good time to switch to the June bug setup. When I get my line reeled in, I see my anchovy is gone. I switch my rig over to a setup just like Jake's and then hunt around for a June bug. There's none on the lantern, but I find one crawling from the shadows into the lantern's light. I hook the June bug and move over to the edge of the aqueduct and announce

"I'm getting one, too."

Dad comes over to stand by me as I aim my cast for the same spot as Jake hit. If there's one, there's got to be two or more. I've seen schools of bluegill and schools of trout. Stripers, they must be in schools, too.

I make my cast.

It's gotten too dark to see the June bug or the bobber. I hear the splash but all I see is the line that goes from my rod tip toward the water's surface.

I take up some slack in the line and watch it intently as it nears the point where Jake's strike happened. With my left hand I have a firm grip on the rod, ready to set the hook. The reel crank is in my right hand and I'm just as ready to start cranking on it immediately after I've set the hook.

The line keeps moving right to left. Straight out from me is twelve o'clock. The line is moving in counterclockwise motion and I'm sure that between one o'clock and eleven o'clock there's a big striper waiting for his June bug dinner.

I watch and wait, ready as I can be, as the line sweeps from two o'clock to one o'clock, to twelve, to eleven. When the line reaches ten o'clock I decide it's time for a second try.

As I reel in without a bite, I hear dad tell Jake we forgot our fish bucket. Mrs. Tano says she is ready to go home and offers to let Jake borrow her second rope with stringer. I'm thinking my second cast with new bait will be my lucky cast. While I'm about to catch the next big one I hear Jake and Mrs. Tano's walking over to her site to get her rope and stringer.

My line is now back in the water, but I glance to see what they are doing. Jake has already put his striper on the stringer. He has the stinger in his right hand and the coiled rope is in his left. Mrs Tano has her pole in one hand and her own striper in her other hand. She doesn't have a tackle box because her fishing vest carries most everything she needs.

I turn my attention back to fishing, but I hear them walk back. As Mrs. Tano walks past, she says "Good night. " to all of us, and to me "Good luck, Bill".

Still intently watching my line, I answer "Goodnight, Mrs. Tano!".

Again my line gets to the ten o'clock mark without any action. I reel it in, remembering how just last summer I caught that rainbow trout on my third cast into the Kern River. My third try will work.

Before I make my next cast, I look to see what Jake is doing. His pole is still on the ground by the lantern, but he is standing at his pole holder. He ties one end of the rope to the holder. He double checks the other end is secured to the stringer and his fish is well attached to the stringer. Then he does a soft, underhand cast of the fish so it will just make it to the water. Putting the fish in the aqueduct water will keep it alive until we are ready to take it home.

With his fish safe and secure, he turns toward the lantern and says "I'm going June bug hunting again." I turn back to the aqueduct and make my lucky, sure catch third cast. Nothing by ten o'oclock, again. By the time I get my line reeled in, Jake is ready to go again. As I'm checking my June bug is still alive, he steps up next to me and says "My turn" and he makes his cast with a new, smaller June bug.

Jake and I spend the next 30 minutes trying to hook another big one. We each have the same setup as what worked for Jake. We take turns casting, first right in the striper's home base, then anyplace within the ballpark. We only stop long enough to find and attach a new June bug if the current one is dead. We get nothing. No hits, no runs, no bites.

When Jake's third June bug is dead, he decides to give up his turn to go check on his striper, but I keep trying. As I keep fishing, Jake takes his unlucky June bug off the hook and chucks it. He removes the hook, weight and bobber and puts all of them in the tackle box. He breaks down his rod to its two pieces and lays them next to the box. He goes over and sits beside his rod holder. He sits there, holding the rope that leads down to his fish on the stringer, while he watches his striper wobble around at the water's edge.

A few minutes later dad asks, "You boys ready to go home?"

Without a word, Jake gets up, grabs the stringer rope and starts to pull it up. I've caught nothing. Even though I'm skunked again, I'm ready to go, too. I bring my line in and disassemble everything. Dad does the same thing. He closes the tackle box and folds up his lawn chair.

"Bill, bring the lantern."

I have my pole pieces in one hand and grab the lantern handle with the other. Dad has his pole, the tackle box and his chair. Jake has his pole and his fish. We head for the car.

Jake's in front, holding his fish out in front of himself like it's a lantern and he's heading into a cave. Dad walks next to me. In a quiet voice he says

"He's mighty proud of that fish"

"Yep, it's his biggest" I reply.

"You know he wouldn't even have caught it if you hadn't seen that first strike".

"Yeah, I guess.."

It took a couple seconds for that to sink in, then I looked up to my dad. He was looking straight ahead, but I knew that he knew I was smiling just a bit.

We get to the car and dad opens the trunk. We load stuff in. Jake has taken his fish off the stringer and it now holding it by the lower lip.

"Dad?" he says.

"Bill, bring the lantern next to me." Dad says.

I set my rod in the trunk and move closer to him. He starts rummaging around in the trunk until he sees the edge of an empty Wonder bread plastic bag. He pulls it out from under the wicker picnic basket mom leaves in the trunk all summer long. Dad opens the bag and turns toward Jake. Jake lifts his still-alive, still-wagging striper up over the opening and then lets it sink down into the bag. The bag is big enough that Jake ties a half square knot to keep it closed. Then he sets the bread bag in the trunk, next to his fishing pole. We all three stand there and look at it for a minute as the white Wonder bread plastic bag slowly withers and wiggles, as if there's a batch of confused dough caught inside, trying to break out.

Dad has gone and opened his car door so we have light inside the car. He yells to us "Let's go, boys. Put out the lantern and close the trunk."

When we get home we unload all our gear and take it to the garage. Jake puts his fish, along with the anchovies, into the garage freezer. It's late and we are tired, none of us think about cleaning the fish before freezing it.

The next day I wake up and see Jake's bed is empty. I figure he is already at the breakfast table, excitedly telling mom about his striper, between bites of pancakes. He is there alright. He is working on a stack of pancakes, but he is calmly recounting last night.

"We saw Mrs. Tano. She had a nice striper. TJ was there with his dad."

"Did you guys catch anything ?" mom asks.

"Dad and Bill were skunked again, but I caught a striper."

I stand in the kitchen doorway, waiting for his big recounting to start, but he's done talking. He goes back to his pancakes. Mom starts to ask him a question, but she sees me, comes over and gives me a hug.

"Good morning. Skunked again ?" she asks. I nod.

"How about some pancakes, then ? How many?"

As I dropped into my chair I answer "Three, please".

Over the next couple weeks Jake is surprisingly quiet about his big catch. It's the kind of story any kid would love to tell all his friends and family, but Jake doesn't bring it up. Something else is strange, too. Jake passes up a couple chances to go play some pick up baseball games with me and the guys. He always plays baseball with us.

I'd grab my glove and ball and then go looking for him around the house and outside. A couple times, when I got near the garage I could hear Jake talking inside. Whenever I went inside to see if he wanted to go play ball, I'd see him standing over by the far wall, near the freezer. Mom and dad's lawn chairs would be set up in the middle of the garage and Jake would be facing the chairs. Jake would have his backpack at his feet and he seemed to be talking to the chairs, making a speech to them. When I first saw this I just assumed he was working on his birthday speech.

Jake doesn't just ask for things, he presents mom and dad with an argument for why he deserves the gift and how it will improve his life, and theirs, too. His birthday was still weeks away but I figured he already knew what he wanted and was honing his plea. Still, it surprised me that whenever I found him working on his speech, he passed on joining us for some baseball.

In early September we are back to school. My sixth grade teacher is Mrs. Howe. Jake and TJ are in Mrs. Morris's fifth grade class. I had her, too, and she is okay. Back when I had her, we did Show and Tell Wednesday, Thursday and Friday of the first week of school, right after lunch. Each day, about 8 kids would get to talk for up to 5 minutes on whatever they brought.

Jake and I are walking to school on our first Thursday back.

"Are you guys doing Show and Tell this week?" I ask.

"Yep. Today is my day" Jake replies.

"What're you showing?"

"Something ..." Jake answers too seriously.

"Great. As long as it's something and not nothing" I say.

I know my little brother can be as tight lipped and stubborn as an angry clam so I just walk the last block to school without another word. He is silent, too.

When we get through the school gate I turn towards some of my friends. "Bill, wait for me after school." Jake calls out in a younger, less serious, voice.

I didn't see this part of the June bug story when it first happened, but I heard about it from multiple people. I heard part of it from TJ during the afternoon recess.

I loved my brother back then and I love him now. I don't doubt that what people told me was the truth, because Jake told me the whole story, just once, on the walk home from school that day.

Like all the kids that live around us, we cut through Kennedy Park going to and from school. The park had the usual stuff, a couple picnic tables, a baseball field, a tall, metal slide and a set of four swings. As Jake and I walk past the big swing set on our way home, I say

"TJ told me you showed a June bug for Show and Tell. He said your Show and Tell was the best."

"My Show and Tell was the best. I practiced it for weeks. Want to hear it? I can tell it right now. You can sit in the swing and listen."

Without waiting for an answer, Jake sets down his backpack, then sets his feet about shoulder width apart, extends his arms downward and gives them a little shake. It looks like he's getting ready to do an Elvis impression. I take a seat in one of the swings.

Before Jake can start, our neighbors, Rebecca, who is in Jake's class, and Ruby, her younger sister, walk by. Ruby says

"Hi Jake, watcha doing?"

"I'm giving my Show and Tell to Bill. Want to hear it ?"

Rebecca giggles a bit, probably because she's seen it already. Ruby asks

"Is it the June bug one?"

Jake rolls his eyes and answers "Yeah, I guess so."

Now Jake has an audience of three, all of us in swings, facing him as he starts his tale.

"Before lunch I asked Mrs. Morris if I could go last because I figured the kids might have lots of questions for me. She said yes, so I was the final act. I took my whole backpack with me when I walked up. I set it down beside me, just like it is now. Then I started.

"My name is Jake De Young. This summer I did lots of cool, awesome things with my family. We went to a Dodgers game and I got this mini-bat." Jake reaches into his backpack and pulls out the little bat and holds it over his head. "See, it says Dodgers right there." He points to the logo on the glossy, 12 inch wooden bat. "The Dodgers beat the Reds 4-1 and my dad almost caught a foul ball." Jake keeps the bat in his right hand, but as he mentions the foul ball, he reaches out with his left hand and then with his eyes he follows an imaginary line drive that gets past his outstretched arm. He continues " We all had Dodger dogs and took turns listening to Vin Scully call the game on our little radio" Jake puts the bat away, then continues.

"And we went camping at Pismo Beach. My mom and I found two sand dollars on the beach" He pulls two of the shells from his backpack and holds them over his head, one in each hand. As he talks, he makes eye contact with each of us. "They're whole sand dollars, nothing broken or anything. Mom's going to frame them." He puts the dollars away.

"And", he pauses. "Best of all, I went fishing at the aqueduct with my dad and my brother. Our friend, Mrs. Tano, was there. We saw this scary, glassy-eyed man chopping". Jake does a couple big windmill motions with his right arm. His right hand is the knife blade, popping as it hits his upturned left hand. "We thought he was chopping anchovies for bait, but he was really chopping and chunking a snake, a *Garter snake* " Now he extends his left hand towards us "and he offers us the snake head as bait."

Rebecca and Ruby let out "Eeews". Jake continues "We didn't want any snake parts. Later on we talked with TJ and his dad. They were going after catfish. My brother Bill got to light the lantern. And then we heard this gigantic fish jump."

Now Jake reaches into his backpack and pulls out the Wonder bread bag. I'm pretty sure I know what's in there, but his classmates must have been curious when they first saw it. Ruby asks "You caught a loaf of bread ?"

Jake ignores her and unties the bag. Along with practicing the talking, Jake must have worked on showing off the fish. Once he had the bag open, he peers inside it and sticks his right arm down inside it. As he is reaching into the bag, he is lowering it, too. By the time he has gripped the fish, he is bent over, with the bag at about his knee level. He looks up, towards us, and as he starts to straighten up he slowly says

"And .. I .. caught .. this."

He starts to reveal his striper. I notice that as he is pulling the fish out of the bag, he is also lifting the bag. This draws out the whole process, making the fish look even bigger. The silence adds to the drama. I'm sure this impressed a lot of his classmates.

Jake's hand is at his eye level by the time he has the fish completely out of the bag. The fish's mouth is wide open and Jake is holding it by its lower lip. He sets the bag down so he can use both hands to hold his fish. He balances it in both hands, at his shoulder level, and bounces it up and down a little bit, to show that it is big and heavy.

"Is that real?" Ruby asks skeptically.

"Yep, it's a 7 lbs 10 oz striper. Dad says it took me nearly 10 minutes to land him. I caught him with.."

Rebecca says to Ruby "Here's where Gregory asked the question."

"What? What question?" I ask.

"Gregory asked 'How far inside the fish can you see?'"

"Oh, that's a good question. How far, Jake ?" I ask, not so innocently.

Jake turns the fish so it is facing him. He looks into its mouth. He squints "Not far".

"That's not how you did it in class." Rebecca says.

"I'm not doing that again." Jake quickly replies.

"Come on. That's the best part." Rebecca says.

Ruby joins in "Come on, Jake. I didn't get to see it."

"You said you were retelling it so you have to retell all of it." I pile on.

Using both hands, Jake lifts the fish so the mouth is at his eye level and the tail is slightly higher. It looks like he has a fish telescope, scanning just above the horizon. Jake's face is

kind of pinched up and he is squinting even more as he looks
into the fish's mouth. He starts to move the fish back, away
from his face, then something brown and roundish rolls out
of the fish's mouth, bounces off Jake's nose and falls on to
the sand in front of Jake.

Jake lets out a yell of surprise. Ruby and Rebecca both
let out

"Eeewww, gross! What is it?" and pull their feet up close
to their swings, as if they're afraid the mysterious brown
thing is coming after their toes. Since TJ had already told me
about Jake's show and tell, I know the brown thing is the
very June bug Jake used to catch the striper. TJ said some of
the class laughed it up when the fish spit out the June bug.
Others made the same kind of noise that Ruby and Rebecca
just did. TJ told me in class Jake let out a yell when the bug
fell out of the fish, but then Jake calmly and coolly picked it
up.

Jake scans the ground and sees the June bug. He moves
the fish to just his right hand at waist level. With his left
hand he picks up the June bug, briefly looks at it, then holds
it up over his head, like one of his sand dollars. In a slow,
clear voice, like a boxing ring announcer at a championship
fight, he says

"Ladies and gentlemen, this is the very June bug I used
to catch and defeat this magnificent striper."

Jake lifts the striper to chest height as he says this last
part. He pauses and lowers his hand holding the June bug.
He lowers the fish, too. I think he has lost his place or
forgotten what he wants to say. After a second, he looks
down at his June bug, then he tosses the June bug up in the
air, like it is a juggling ball. All four of us watch the June bug
fly up, in front of Jake's face, then make a U-turn towards
the ground. It looks like the June bug is going to fall to the
ground or maybe land on Jake's right shoe. As the June bug

falls past Jake's shoulder, he adjusts the striper just a fraction of an inch right before the bug falls into the fish's gapping mouth. A perfect swish, the basketball players would say. His striper has once again swallowed the June bug. Jake looks to us, smiles, quickly winks and takes a bow, holding the striper high in his right hand, the way a magician would hold his top hat. Ruby giggles and claps. Rebecca joins the clapping, too. Jake straightens up and has a big, beaming smile on his face. He takes a second bow, then picks up the Wonder bread bag and puts the striper back in the bag and the bag in his backpack.

"That's it. That's my show and tell. Mrs. Morris said I was very entertaining, but there was no time for any more questions" Jake says as he slings his backpack over his shoulder and starts walking the rest of the way home. We hop out of our swings and join him. As we near the girl's house, Rebecca says "My show and tell is going to be about the Saturday I helped grandma sell antiques at the swap meet. She gave me a turquoise necklace for helping her.

"I want to help grandma" Ruby says as they turn onto their own sidewalk.

"You're too young" Rebecca automatically replies, sounding much like a mom.

Jake and I continue down the street. I ask him
"Is that what you were practicing in the garage ?"
"Yep"
"Did you know the June bug was still inside the striper?"
"You know how Mrs. Morris makes us sit in last name alphabetic order for lunch?" Jake asks, ignoring my question.

"Yeah, she made us do that last year, too." I reply.

"I guess I'll be sitting next to Gregory Devoy for the rest of this year" and with that, Jake bolts towards the front door, leaving me with my question.

Now we are twenty four years later and many miles apart, but whenever I first hear Jake's voice on the phone, it is those two "June bug" images, the evening he landed his striper and his performance in the park, that instantly flash in my mind. We don't always talk about his striper or June bugs, but we always talk about dad and about fishing. When we finish our talks and I hang up the phone, I usually think about that September day in Kennedy park, seeing him beaming with pride, the fish in hand as he winks and takes a bow. It reminds me why I love my brother.

Big Savings

I always wondered about those commercials where someone claimed to save hundreds of dollars on their car insurance. How could rates be so different for a person. Well, here's my story. I was working late one night in the library when she walked in. Oh wait, that's a different story. Let's get back to the insurance story. Just a little over three years ago I got a speeding ticket. My insurance company waited a few months before raising my rate. Jump ahead to when she's checking out some books. I mean, jump ahead to my policy coming up for renewal this month. I call my company to check the rates and in the process I find out my rates are raised for another 11 months because of my heavy foot. So I ask her if she likes goofy fiction without much plot, I mean I call another company and because my ticket is over 3 years old they can give me a rate that's hundreds less. So she laughs, but I don't know if it's a courtesy laugh or something more. For about 2 seconds I think I should just stay with my current company, but then I realize that's stupid. There's a nice opportunity right in front of me. And that's how I met Flo.

Sweeping It Up – Tangina's Tale

I woke in a good mood this morning, almost chipper. I knew I had my regular 9am group meeting but nothing with business partners today so I could dress casual and go lighter on the makeup, too. I looked outside and saw just a few clouds so I elected to ride my bike into work. It's a pleasant 35 minute ride, with the first and last parts on city streets and the middle 20 minutes or so on a bike path. The air was fresh and clean and perfectly cool. I cruised along without a worry.

I like cycling, especially on an early morning like this one. The smell of earth at dawn and the damp air on my cheeks reminds me of the two wonderful years I spent training and exercising racehorses at Golden Gate Fields racetrack. The racetrack is near U.C. Berkeley, where I was a student at the time.

Of course I didn't just show up at Berkeley and get admitted into their computer science program, nor did I just show up at Golden Gate Fields and get offered thoroughbreds to ride. In both cases it took hard work and perseverance. For Berkeley it was my high school grades and my second set of SAT scores that got me in. For Golden Gate Fields, it was my three straight years as the Fresno Country Rodeo Junior Barrel Racing Champion, along with my jockey-like size. It also helped that my uncle, who trained horses and riders in the Fresno area, knew Gerry, one of the trainers working at the racetrack.

In my freshman and sophomore years at Berkeley I worked a few mornings a week at the track during the race seasons. Most of the time I just did cleanup work. Clean out the stalls, clean and oil the bridles and saddles, straighten up the tack room and keep it neat was about 90 percent of my time there. Gerry insisted on a kind of orderliness I didn't completely understand at the time but over the years since then I have come to realize keeping things neat and tidy simplifies my life and suits me well as a lifestyle.

I never rode in any races, but once in a while I got to take horses on their training runs and, afterward, cool them down. That made it all worthwhile. I loved being around such strong, intelligent, beautiful animals. I was lucky to have those two years, back when my school work was light enough that I could spend time at the track.

I'm ten years out of college and my morning rides into work still put me in a good mood because they remind me of those two years. Today's ride in was no exception, I was enjoying the ride until the very end. When I got into work I saw my water bottle was missing from its carrier on the bike frame. I knew I had filled the bottle with water and set it in the carrier before leaving home. I'd even taken a sip from it when I stopped at the first red traffic light.

The carrier is attached to the bike frame with Velcro strapping. The strapping and carrier were exactly where they should be, on the lower tube of the bike frame, but no water bottle. I was bummed out to see it was missing.

The bottle was a gift from a small hi-tech start-up company, called Carolanne Computing, I worked at almost five years ago. We had a product release party where everyone got a company logo sports bottle. In the after-lunch prize raffle, I won a $25 gift certificate from Big-5 Sporting Goods. I used that certificate to get the water bottle carrier and a pair the biking gloves.

When I started biking into my current job I rode into work with that sports bottle many times without it so much as rattling around while in the carrier. Not only that, but whenever I ride my bike I don't wear headphones or earbuds so I certainly should have heard it today if it fell out of its rack. It was odd for it to be gone, but odd as it seemed, once I was at work I had 15 minutes to get ready for my 9am. I shrugged off the bottle's vanishing act and headed to the company fitness center to shower and change into my work clothes. I got to my meeting a couple minutes late, but so did everyone else.

Not to dwell on the rest of the day's events but they were a bit tougher than usual, starting with that first meeting going an extra 30 minutes, followed by some difficult hallway conversations on the best way to divide up the project going forward. It is always a tricky conversation because we have to decide what work is done by our U.S. team and what work is done by our India team. It took the rest of the morning to resolve the issue. By noon I was really ready for a break from work and a peaceful, quiet lunch.

On days like today I usually walk over to Beenie's shop for a sandwich or a wrap. It's a chance to get some fresh air. Plus, Beenie makes an excellent Ruben and a pretty good chicken Caesar salad wrap. Unfortunately, the weather had gotten worse as the morning went on, with a heavy rain starting to fall just as I stepped outside for my walk. I reluctantly went back inside, got a mediocre burrito from our cafeteria and ate it at my desk while I caught up on email. Around 2:30 my boss, Gabe, stopped by to tell me he had some bad chowder at lunch and was going home sick and feverish. He actually looked like bad chowder.

Before he left he asked me to present our monthly status at the big 3pm program review. It's a two hour meeting, with each of the four teams getting 30 minutes to report on their piece of the program.

I usually attend the meeting, but mostly to listen and take note of any new action items for my team. This time I would be presenting, meaning I'd be talking for about 30 minutes. Gabe left me his four pages of status notes and his eight slide presentation. I had enough time before the meeting to review all of his prep work and to quickly practice my delivery just once.

Because I try to keep my life orderly I don't always handle these unexpected things with grace. Going into the meeting I felt rushed and anxious and unprepared to present. It was a crowded meeting room and to make it worse, Jonathan, the engineering VP, was attending this time. He is a sharp guy and can ask some challenging questions.

I was last to present so I had time to mentally practice my status report a few more times during the meeting. That calmed me down some and helped me get more comfortable with the material, at least until I actually had to present. Right as the previous presenter was finishing, I rushed through my boss's notes one more time, but the presenter finished sooner than I anticpated. When I got called to present I hastily flipped back to the beginning of my boss's notes, but in my haste I accidentally ended up on the second page. I started my presentation with slide one, but was reading from page two notes.

I didn't notice my mistake, but as I was talking something felt wrong. I was just too nervous and overwhelmed to recognize it. About a minute into my presentation someone interrupted with

"Tangina, something is wrong. I think your slides are messed up".

I looked up and saw it was the VP talking to me. I didn't think he knew my name, let alone my nickname. I'm sure I looked at him with stunned silence. In a friendly voice, he said

"Check your slides. They don't jive with what you are saying."

I looked at the projector and saw it was slide one. I looked at my notes and saw it was page two. I realized my foolish error and flipped back to page one. I double checked slide one was on the display and I really was on page one. As confidently as possible I said

"Thanks Jonathan. Let me start over."

For some reason I was much calmer on the restart, maybe because the VP saw my mistake, but didn't make a big deal of it. Whatever the reason, the rest of my status report went smoothly, but it still was a lot of talking for me to do at one time. The only question I got was from Jonathan. He wanted to know if we had figured out the division of project labor. I told him we had just worked it out earlier in the day and my boss wanted to present the plan to Jonathan next week.

When the meeting ended I silently picked up my laptop and my notes, hugged them to my chest and scrammed out of there. When I got back to my desk I did a quick check of email and then called the work day done. I felt worn out and beat down, even a little diminutive. With all the extra talking, by the end of the day my voice had gotten quite weary and it sounded higher pitched than normal.

I headed back to the fitness center to change into my biking clothes. On the walk there I was happy to see the weather had cleared up to about the same state as when I rode into work in the morning. After a tough day, at least I had the relaxing ride home to look forward to.

I don't wear a helmet, but I do tie my hair up. I like that we still have the freedom to ride a bike without a helmet and I take advantage of it. However, because this time of year there are plenty of gnats in the morning and bees and other flying bugs in the afternoon I do wear eye protection. I get kidded a bit about my choice of eye wear protection, but I want something that does the job, something that maximizes the protection zone. For me, that means wearing what some co-workers have described as oversized aviator sunglasses. I don't think they are oversized, I think they are right-sized to do the job. There are too many flying insects out there to wear glasses with "normal" lens. I need the big ones.

I get geared up and head for home.

Because of traffic patterns near work, my ride home is slightly different from my ride to work. There's a lot less traffic on some streets in the morning so I use them on the ride in. In the evening, those streets are busy so I use a different route. The first part of the ride home takes me by the local dump and recycling center. Luckily, I'm on the upwind side of that unhappy potpourri.

While I don't have to suffer the olfactory onslaught, I do occasionally have to dodge various man-made items that either didn't make it to the dump or subsequently escaped from it. Computer keyboards and women's underwear seem to be the most common items that end up in the street gutter of this section of road. I don't know how they end up here but in my years riding this route I've seen at least a half dozen of each. Both are cause for concern.

I know the keyboards can be dangerous because one time I tried to just ride right over one. As you might guess, for a woman I'm a bit below average height and about average weight. At the time I sure thought I had enough mass to keep the keyboard pinned in place as I rode over it. I remember the evening it happened. I had just turned onto the dump street and when I saw the light beige rectangular object laying in the gutter ahead of me I immediate recognized it. It was a cheap keyboard with no ergonomic IQ and probably a missing ESC key. It was one sure to induce carpal tunnel syndrome. I saw it. I recognized it. I disliked it and I wanted to punish it for all the past pain keyboards like it had caused my hands and fingers.

As I approached it I moved most of my weight forward, over my handlebars. I looked down to watch as my front tire climbed over the ¾ inch plastic lip and began to type a path across the keys; spacebar-comma-kl-o. Suddenly, when my front wheel was smashing the 'o' key, the whole keyboard started sliding out from under my center of balance. The plastic mass must have been sitting on top of an oily spot. As it slid, it was taking my front tire out towards the road, towards traffic. Both me and the keyboard were saying "OOOOOOOOO" at the same time. Fortunately, I quickly pulled up on the handlebars and was free of the evil slippery devil. With the pull I got myself back in balance and my front tire landed on solid non-slippery ground. A torque on the pedals and my back tire was quickly across the ugly plastic thing. I was glad to be over and past the foul beast. I didn't even glance back at it.

Since then I just go around the keyboards. The women's underwear are just the opposite of slippery keyboards. They never seem to move no matter how many times I roll over them. Wherever a pair of underwear appears on the roadside, they just stay in the exact place until they are worn away like some kind of indecent roadkill or they get sucked up by a pervert street sweeper. The synthetics survive a lot longer than the cotton ones. The odd thing is they all seem to be about the same size. I wonder if it is one careless woman or women of that size are generally careless. For the record, I'm not that size and I've never lost any of my underwear.

On today's ride home I kept a watchful eye on the gutter ahead of me. I saw neither computer keyboards nor women's underwear, but there were a couple other riders.

Riders I'd not seen before. They were riding slower than me and as I caught up with them I said to them in my still high-pitched voice

"Ya'll mind hanging back? You're jamming my frequency".

They parted and let me through. I rode along the street for a few more minutes.

As I approached the end of the dump road, right before I made the transition to the bike path, I spotted something odd looking against the edge of the curb. When I first saw it I thought it might be a piece of one inch pvc pipe or a painted wooden dowel, with a dish rag or hand towel next to it, but when I pulled up beside it I saw it was something even more out of place. It was one of those modern Swiffer sweeper things!

I picked it up to get a closer look. Not only was the white handle surprisingly unmarked, but the Swiffer head, the business end of it, was amazingly clean, too. I immediately fell in love with this Swiffer, with its unexpected cleanliness, its implied neatness and its aromatic, lemony invitation. I decided I needed it. Even though I had a broom, a mop and a vacuum at home, I would adopt this lonely, abandoned modern cleaning tool and welcome it into my tidy family.

Given all my various riding experiences, I knew I could get it home safely, I'd just hold the end of the Swiffer handle in one hand and set its pole out in front of me so it rested on my bike's handle bars, sort of like I was getting ready to joust. I'd have to ride a bit slower, but it would work.

With my left hand steering and my right hand holding the Swiffer handle, I turned onto the bike path. The bike path is nice because it's away from car traffic, but now, in the early summer it can get overgrown with new, exuberant grasses and weeds lining the pathway. As this excited flora reaches for the sun, some of it leans in from the sides of the path and this makes the path narrower. There's not a lot of traffic on this path so a narrower path is not usually a problem. To avoid the overgrowth I ride down the middle of the path.

I've been making this ride for years so I know it well. Even before they sprout, I can tell you right where the little patch of wild, perennial corn will grow. For at least the last three years there are eight to 12 stalks right at the bottom of the only undulation on the otherwise flat bike path. I always thought corn was supposed to be just an annual, but this wild corn keeps coming back each year in the same spot.

The tallest weeds are about knee high, but all the corn stalks are at least 4 feet tall by now. Two of the stalks already show the beginnings of ears.

As I'm jousting through this forest of weeds and wilderness, headed home, I am feeling much better. The day's work stress is nearly gone. I sit up in the saddle and do a couple shoulder shrugs to work out the last of the stress. In the process of loosening up my neck muscles I notice the clouds have begun to gather up again. Rain is probably just a few minutes away but I still have at least 15 minutes of riding. Since I don't have any rain gear with me I decide to pick up my pace. I accelerate even more as I head down the path's one undulation.

I start getting a speed wobble half way down the slope so I stop pedaling, but that's not enough impedance. Since my right hand is holding the Swiffer I can only apply the brake with my left hand. I really don't want to crash so I put on the brake. Uh-oh, it's the front brake. The one that can help you fly over the front of your bike head first if you apply it too hard too fast. What saves me from flying this time is what dooms me, too. Not only do I apply the brake, but I also take my right foot off the pedal and start dragging it on the ground. My thinking is this will slow me down quicker and with more stability than just using the front brake. With some of my weight shifted onto my foot, I won't go catapulting over my handlebars. It's a good idea until my foot suddenly hits a sandy silt patch. My foot quickly slides out almost perpendicular to my bike and away from my center of balance. My fear of crashing is augmented by a new fear. I fear my right hamstring will get pulled apart because I've started to do a fast, hard slide towards the splits position.

I'm trying to keep control of my bike and my balance. I'm squeezing the brake lever with my left hand. I'm protecting my new Swiffer with my right hand. My left foot is still on the pedal. My right foot is getting away from me and so is my balance. I know from my days as a jockey that sometimes to avoid an uncontrolled hard fall you decide to take a controlled fall you hope is less painful. I lean over towards my right foot and then use my left foot to push off from the bike. That launches me free of my bike, but I'm headed towards a crash on the side of the path. Fortunately, I know how to roll a fall, thus avoiding a hard landing. While I'm in the air I pull my right hand in against my belly, bringing the end of the Swiffer close to me. I use my left hand to lift the Swiffer handle up from the handlebars. I quickly set the Swiffer handle against that area of my body where the collar bone disappears into the right shoulder. The way I'm holding the Swiffer, it must look like I'm pretending to be a soldier with a rifle at right shoulder arms.

With my Swiffer secured, I tuck my head down and arch my shoulders forward. I know the impact is coming. The back side of my right shoulder makes first contact with the ground. As I roll, I feel the pressure of the ground roll across my back, from right shoulder, over the middle of my spine, down to my left kidney and to my left butt cheek. I've done a somersault of sorts and come to rest sitting like a rag doll.

My legs are straight out in front of me and I'm slouched over a bit. Fortunately, nothing is hurting or throbbing, my glasses are still in place and my arms are still in their protective position. I look up at the Swiffer head and see it is still wonderfully clean and unscathed. That wasn't so bad.

When I stand up, the first thing I notice is how surprisingly dirty I've gotten. It's not just my backside, somehow the front of my yellow Live Strong shirt is now unacceptably dirty, too. I carefully set down the Swiffer, leaning it against my downed bike so the Swiffer head is propped up off the ground. I start dusting off my shirt. While I'm brushing myself off as best I can, I inspect the scene to understand what happened. I crashed at the bottom of the undulation. I slid and rolled through the silt and some mud. How did the trail get so muddy ugly since this morning ? I realize it must have gotten there because rain from earlier in the day. The midday rain puddled up at the undulation base and then during the day it mostly evaporated, leaving a terribly messy and obviously dangerous path. Well that won't do, especially when I have this, a Swiffer sweeper. It's made for these ugly situations.

First I grab the Swiffer and then pick up my bike and set it on its kickstand. Then I start sweeping the ugliness off the path. I'm excited to see what the much advertised cleaning device is really capable of. I quickly realize there's so much dirt to wipe away I'll need more water than whatever inherently resides in the Swiffer. I keep the sweeping going with my right arm while I reach over to get my water bottle from my bike. When my hand doesn't find it I glance over and I see just the empty carrier. My baby is gone ! I'd been so busy all day I hadn't even thought about my missing water bottle. Now the angst comes rushing back to me. In frustration I yell

"Daah!! Where are you water bottle? Come back. Come back to me."

I'm mad, madder than I should be. The combination of realizing my water bottle is gone and the frustration of crashing in the dirty, muddy spot has gotten to me. I'm so mad, from the bike I unvelcro the rack just to hear the sound of it ripping. While I keep sweeping with my right hand, I use my left hand to pull the carrier off the frame tube. Holding it by the strap, I lift it to the sky.

I start to yell something at the heavens but I immediately forget what it is because I'm fascinated by what I see. Gray clouds, just out of my reach, are swirling in a tight circle, spinning, with pulses of light flashing within the clouds. It's like watching a satellite image of a terrifying gulf coast hurricane on a tv that's floating right above me. I've never seen clouds so dense nor so close to the ground and me. I'm mesmerized by the action and impressed by the nearness of it.

As I'm watching this mini hurricane, something pulls on my left arm and it draws my attention. I see the end of the Velcro strap is still in my raised left hand, but instead of leading to an empty carrier hanging from the other end of the strap, the strap is now stretched up into a region of the swirling clouds. The rack has disappeared into a bright spot in the clouds and something up there is tugging on the strap, tugging on my arm, trying to steal my rack.

I'm very much freaked out by this and quite speechless. I can't think of a single plausible reason for the rack to be pulled up into the clouds. I hear myself gasp and then there's silence for a second as I think about this oddness, what I want and how to get it. I'm not going to lose my rack. As a matter of fact, I'm keeping my rack...and I want my water bottle back, too. I hear myself say something bizarre, yet familiar. "Carolanne, Carolanne come to the light. Do you hear me! Come to light. Come to me right now!" and I instinctively pull down on the strap. I begin to pull it back, but only an inch more of the strap is exposed when whatever is on the other end pulls even stronger. I'm not giving up. I let go of the Swiffer in my right hand so I can get both hands pulling on the strap. With my right hand I grab the strap right above my left hand. I tighten my grip like I'm holding the reins of an unruly thoroughbred. Using all my strength and weight, I pull on the strap. In a determined voice I shout into the clouds "Carolanne, come to mommy right now."

I'm pulling down so hard, I've almost lifted myself off the ground when the resistance suddenly and completely releases. It catches me off guard and I can't get my feet back under me properly. I lose my balance and fall over for the second time today. I land pretty hard on my backside.

This time I'm stunned by hitting the ground and by the events that just happened. I lay on the bike path with my eyes closed so I can regroup, gather myself and take a physical inventory of myself to make sure nothing is too hurt. My tailbone is aching, but not too bad. Everything else seems fine physically, but I'm having a hard time believing what just happened.

I've heard of magnetic storms, but I'm not sure what they really are. The rack is metal. Maybe the storm was just a super intense magnetic storm that grabbed the rack and tried to pull it out of my hands. Maybe, but I don't think so.

I open my eyes and the first thing I see is the angry clouds. They have slowed their swirling and flashing. They are not so angry looking now and they are floating up towards the rest of the clouds.

"Good" I say as I get back to my feet and adjust my glasses. I realize both my hands are empty. During my fall I must have let go of the strap. I look around for it and the rack, hoping that whatever strangeness pulled the rack into the clouds didn't damage it. I figure if the rack and strap are okay then all I'll need is another water bottle. As I look around, I laugh at myself for having thought Carolanne could have been held prisoner up in those clouds.

I look to my left and to my right. I turn around in a circle as I check the path. I don't see strap or rack. I thought I won the battle when I pulled the strap free, but it looks like I lost everything today; water bottle, rack and strap.

Disappointed, I adjust my glasses again and then dust myself off once more. Of course I still want to take the Swiffer home so I go to pick it up. The handle is long enough that when it fell onto the path it actually laid all the way across the path. The head was still in the dirty silty gunk. The end of the handle has disappeared into the weeds on the other side of the path. When I bend down to grab the handle I am surprised to see a piece of the strap nearly hidden in the same weeds.

"There you are" I say as I reach for the strap. When I pull it out it comes with a tangle of weeds on the other end. Even with the ball of weeds hiding the other end of the strap, I can tell by the weight of the thing that the rack is still there with the strap. Great, I have my carrier back. I tear away the ball of weeds to see that not only is the rack there, but miraculously Carolanne is back in the rack. "Carolanne" I cry out as I hug it to my chest. "Your back! Mommy missed you so much!"

I am full of happiness and joy. As I'm hugging Carolanne, I'm twisting side to side a little bit, too. I realize I can hear water splashing around. I stop my twisting and hold Carolanne out in front of me. Yep, she's retaining water, and, to my surprise, the water is warm. I can tell because Carolanne is warm in my grip. It is about two-thirds full. I'm not even sure it had that much when I left home with it this morning, but I quickly realize it should be plenty, and for any cleanup everyone knows warm water will be better than just ambient stuff.

After I reattach the carrier to my bike, I pick up the Swiffer and I get to work. The job must be finished. Using Carolanne, I soak the head of my Swiffer and then spray some water directly on the silty area. The moisture really makes a big difference. The silt starts coming right up and in about 2 minutes of sweeping I have the trail looking pretty darn good.

There's still a small patch left to clean when the Swiffer starts to leave streaks of silt behind. I stop sweeping so I can inspect its cleaning cloth. The Swiffer's contact portion is completely dark brown, poor thing. Fortunately, Carolanne still has about 6 ounces of warm water. I figure that is enough to rinse off the cloth. I hold the Swiffer's head off to the side of the path and use the water from Carolanne to wash a lot of the dirt off of the head. It's not the pristine white it was just a 25 minutes ago, but it definitely is cleaner than when I just inspected it. The dark, dirty brown has lightened to a mild beige.

I spray the last bit of water onto the dirt patch on the path and make one more sweeping pass over it. The whole area is looking tv commercial quality clean. The clouds overhead have cleared away enough to let the sun dry up the little bit of moisture left on the path. While I'm admiring my handiwork, I hear some riders approaching. I look up and see some of the cyclist I passed early on. I move to the side of the path and then turn to them as they approach. I stand as upright and tall as I can, at my full 4 feet, 8 and a half inch height, proudly holding my Swiffer in my right hand,

Carolanne in my left hand, with my tinted aviator sunglasses perfectly in place and my hair piled and pinned up on the top of my head. I pronounce to them as they ride by

"This path.." I tap the path with the Swiffer handle a couple times. "...is now clean."

Naturally, all the riders bow their heads down to inspect the path and, I feel quite certain, to show respect to the woman who cleaned the path and exorcised the demons of dirt and messiness.

After they pass by, I hop on my bike and make the rest of my ride home without any problems or poltergeists.

The Marble King

We played marbles. Kids from my block and the nearby blocks played in the dirt driveway next to my parent's house. Once in a while there would be a game at the playground two streets over, but the dirt in the neighbor's driveway was the best set up. It was hard packed underneath, but there was just enough fine dust on top so that we could draw game lines in it.

Kids were always trying to invent new games, with new rules that they thought would work for them, but mostly we played Fish.

Everyone knew the Fish rules. First we draw an outline of a fish, sort of like your basic goldfish outline. Then, about 8 feet from the fish, someone draws a lag line. It's just a straight line you stand behind when it's your turn to shoot. Next, each of us puts in the same number of marbles, usually six. We space about half the marbles along the outline and the other half get grouped together in the center of the fish. Every couple of inches along the fish outline there would be a cat's eye or an aggie or a bumble bee. In the middle of the fish's body would be a hodgepodge of marbles tightly packed together. The game was simple. When it was your turn, you stand at the lag line and toss your shooter towards the fish. If your marble goes inside the fish you lose your turn, but if the marble is outside the fish, that's where you take your first shot. With your shooter marble, you would shoot from outside the fish. Any marble you knocked outside the fish, you kept. If your shooter marble stayed inside the fish outline, you got to shoot again. Once you didn't knock any marble outside the fish, your turn was done and the next kid went. The idea was that during your turn, you knock as many marbles out of the fish as possible, while still keeping your shooter inside the fish perimeter. If you put 6 marbles into the game, then you wanted to shoot good enough to get your 6 back, and maybe a few more.

Over any given summer month, we'd play at least 40 games. My recollection is that no one lost all of their marbles and no one won all the marbles. Kids would have a good day. Kids would have a bad day. One time I lost my lucky green cat's eye shooter, but the next week I won a slightly oversized bumble bee that became my new shooter and helped me replenish my marble bag.

One evening towards the end of the summer of '71, the Marble King appeared amongst us. Now you might think that the King was someone a few years older than the rest of us kids, with an oversized shooting thumb and a few profanities we'd only heard our dads utter, but that was not the case at all. When we first saw him, we didn't recognize him as the Marble King. We knew him simply as Low, the kindly old man who lived across the street from my parent's house. Us kids all knew Low for two things. He "mowed" his front lawn using hand sheers. He would be out there on his hands and knees, working the sheers as he slowly cut about 5 inches of grass at a time. It would take him a few days to complete trimming his front lawn. He never used a lawn mower or hired one of us kids to mow his lawn. Any one of us could have mowed it nice and neat in about 15 minutes, with either a push mower or a powered one. It would take him a couple days to sheer it all. He must have gotten something more out of the slow, laborious work than the physical effort because he continued to do it for at least the 12 years we lived across the street from him. I'm certain he had the means to take care of his lawn in a less labor intensive way.

Low's other claim to fame was paying kids for good grades. Some parents gave their kids money if they got good grades on their report card. Some parents didn't. What some of us knew was that if we showed Low our report card, we'd probably get some dime-store candy money from him. He'd pay you a quarter for each A, a dime for each B and a nickel for each C. I was not a great student, but I did well enough to get excited about showing my report card to Low.

Oh man, the sheer joy of having half a dozen coins jiggling around inside my pants pocket as I biked to the corner store was just amazing. Knowing I could buy any candy bar, any ice cream bar, or any bubble gum I wanted was a euphoric cloud 9 experience.

None of us had ever seen Low play marbles or even thought about him as a player. He was older than our own parents. His kids were grown up and out of the house. He walked slow and when he turned to look at something he had to twist at the shoulders because he had a bad neck.

He never talked marbles with us before that day. All the times he reviewed our report cards he always asked about school and teachers and how our moms and dads were doing. Marbles were never part of the conversation. On that day he even showed up at the driveway empty handed. He just quietly walked up to the game and watched us play for a while.

When Low asked if he could play, us kids just looked at him in stunned silence. An adult, an old dude, playing marbles ? After a couple seconds he says he has to borrow someone's shooter. We look around at each other, trying to make sense of the situation, each of us wondering if we want to give up one of our shooters. "Shane, you got a nice bumble bee shooter. Can I give it a try?" he asks me. I look at my bumble bee in my hand. What can I do? He's an adult and I'm just a kid in cut off shorts and a Mohawk haircut (thanks to my dad). I can't say no to him, but as I hand over my favoritest shooter ever to him, I feel like I'm saying good bye to my best friend.

Once Low has my shooter in his hand, everyone seems to realize we got a game going on. Low asks "Who's turn is it?" and Junior tells Low to just go ahead and take a turn. Among our pack of marble gamers, Junior is the boldest player and first talker. He'll go play kids on other blocks, kids he has never met. Most of us can't go past 3rd street, but Junior's parents let him roam all the way from first street to 12th. He plays the 12th streeters once in a while.

Low takes my bumble bee and rolls it around in his hand. He sizes it up. He steps behind the lag line and leans toward the fish. When he extends his arm out to take his lag, it seems like his hand is practically over the fish. His gentle release of my bumble bee sends it on a short flight that ends when it lands just a few inches from yellow aggie Junior had set on the outline of the fish's tail. With that, Low slowly gets down to game level. He's on his hands and knees, just like when he trims the grass. As he gets his hand in position to take his first shot, we are silent in our curiosity, not knowing what to expect or how to react. We all notice that the back side of his hand is not normal. His knuckles are way oversized. They are all bubbled up and swollen, like someone took some poorly mixed concrete and slapped tablespoon of it onto each joint and then hastily patted it down. I'm surprised at myself for having not noticed this before.

At that age I was too young to recognize the ravages of arthritis, so I just figured the bulges were because he'd built up hand muscle from all the lawn sheering he did. His hand was so swollen I was afraid he was going to simply crush my bumble bee shooter like it was a dried up dirt clod or he would shoot it with such force it would skip all the way across the driveway and end up in the fenced and Doberman-guarded front yard of Ms Archibald. As Low got ready for his first shot, I had plenty trepidation and concern for my bumble bee.

While I was chewing on my concern, Low was lining up his shot. When he launched the shooter, it didn't disintegrate. It didn't zoom across the driveway. Instead, it had a head-on collision with Junior's yellow aggie that was on the fish outline. Low's shot knocked the aggie outside the fish and he got the bumble bee to stop inside the fish. Low just won his first marble and he was going to get another shot.

Junior says "Nice shot" and a couple of the other kids do, too. I don't say anything because I was hoping to get the yellow aggie now in Low's possession. I am down my favorite shooter and one marble I wanted and I haven't even taken a turn. I was thinking he just got lucky and that he will miss his next shot and that will be it. I'll get my shooter back and with 29 marbles still in the game I'll have a chance to break even.

Oh, but Low became the Marble King that day. On his first turn, he knocked out 9 marbles. None of us, in all our games had ever knocked out more than 6 in one turn. Was Low the marble hustler that drifted into our town and our game? He nearly cleaned us out. After his 9 marble run, Junior was next. He managed to knock out one marble. Dale got 1 on his turn, Johnny got nothing on his turn and Nick got 2. Everyone, including me, silently agreed that Low was taking my turn. I guess since he was using my shooter he was taking my turn. I stood and watched it all.

When it got back to Low there were 18 marbles still in the game. By then we knew his first turn was not luck. We knew if he went on another 9 marble run, everyone else would come up short. But we were all so fascinated by the spectacle of his dexterity and precision, we had to watch and hope that he would go on another long run.

Low started off his second turn just like his first one. He knocks out a blue cat's eye and his shooter stays inside the fish. He gets his second, third and fourth marbles with no problem. He was getting more accurate and confident with each shot. He pops out five through nine. After his ninth shot he pauses. "Junior, what's the record for most marbles in one turn?" "Aaaah, it was six until today, but you just set a new record of 9...sir."

As Low lined up for his tenth shot he said "Records are meant to be broken" and a green cat's eye is next to go into Low's winning pile. He didn't stop there. He went on for another 7 shots. In pool hall terms, he practically ran the table. His record run was up to 17 and there was just one marble left to win.

Low might as well just pick it up and put it in his pile. We all know it will be his soon as he flicks the bumble bee at that last survivor. "This is it" Junior says in a defeated voice. Low had a bead on the last marble when we all hear the front screen door of his house bang closed. Low's wife is walking over towards us so we all stopped to wait for her.

She gets to the game and says to Low "Honey, your daughter is on the phone. She has a plumbing question for you." Low replies "Okay". He sets down the bee, stands up and dusts himself off and starts to walk back towards his house. Just like that, he's leaving. He is empty handed as he goes. His wife starts to follow him but then she stops and looks at each of us. She must of seen the sadness and pain in our faces. She's a girl, but maybe she understands we all just lost our marbles. She looks at the game and sees a big pile of marbles next to where Low was. "Low's?" she asks as she points at the pile. We all give sad nods. Junior manages a "Yes, ma'am."

"Well, I guess you boys better just keep your marbles. He's got so many already he thinks he's the Marble King." She gives a little hiccup laugh as if the idea of wanting to be the Marble King is somehow funny. After a pause, she turns to her house and follows Low back inside.

You Ever...Moses

Have you ever woken up in the corner booth of a Denny's or IHOP and realized the girl you thought you broke up with earlier in the night is telling you how your brother looks like Ric Ocasek from The Cars and your mind starts to play "Dust in the Wind" and you think "That's Kansas, not The Cars" and a waitress appears and sets a giant strawberry waffle in front of you? The whip cream is mounded up like a pyramid and you think "Those poor slaves. Thank God for Moses" and if you eat all that waffle it will be like setting the slaves free so, even though it's mostly whip cream, you pick up both your fork and your knife and you dig in for the slaves, cutting off blocks of frothy whiteness and finding your mouth, deconstructing. Then she's talking again, telling you how her Saint Bernard sort of looks like Meatloaf and you pretend to listen because you don't remember what state you are in or if your car is automatic or stick. The waffle is gone and the peoples are freed. You smile at your good deed and look across the table. She gives you a sly smile as she reaches first for the ticket and then into her purse for cash. It's your fight or flight or surrender time. While you can't decide, she finds your hand that is glued to the sticky tabletop. Hers is warm and natural and reminds you of the time the two of you walked barefooted on the San Diego beach, and it's decided. You find yourself standing with her, next to the cash register while some transactional conversation happens between her and the white shirt. Beside the register is a toothpick dispenser and next to it is a little model sports car candy holder full of red and white mints. While you hum "Candy-o, I need you so" she pulls you out the door and into the night.

Have You Ever...Great White

Have you ever been relaxing in your '04 Corolla at your favorite breakfast restaurant parking lot, having your favorite breakfast ; rotating muffins, with ham gasket , egg piston, and plastic cheese o-ring sandwich, and you realized the sandwich isn't supposed to have that fishy taste but then, after watching a couple gulls scare off some morning doves, you remember that last night you had an anchovy milkshake and sardine French fries on the beachside patio of Peg Leg Polly's while listening to the best of Great White, including "Once Bitten, Twice Shy" and the fishy taste is really just the smell of the cloth Peg Leg napkin you are still wearing like a pirate's do-rag so you think "mystery solved", finish your sandwich and drive on to work singing "my my my" ?

Have You Ever...Peeps

Have you ever been at the local pizzeria, enjoying a slice and a beverage, when you notice a woman in a completely white sweat suit walk past the restaurant's front window and then you see she has an Easter basket, not a purse that looks like an Easter basket, but an actual Easter basket, with the nest of confetti grass and some colorful, plastic eggs so you decide to check if she has a pink nose or two, long, pointy ears and while you are checking her face she licks something yellow off two of her fingers and you think "peeps!", which reminds you of that time your mom left the kitchen to take a call so it was just you and your older brother dyeing the hard boiled Easter eggs and your brother tried to get you to drink some of the purple egg dye with a "It'll color your tongue and your pee will be purple" and that sounds kind of cool to you so pick up the bowl and just as it touches your lips you hear your mom shout "Don't drink that! It'll turn your pee purple" so now, when the pizzeria waitress asks if you want more grape soap you give her a quick "no thanks" as you slide out of the booth to go next door to Walmart for your own yellow, not purple, peeps after a quick pit stop to make sure it's still the amber it should be?

Have You Ever...Sushi

Have you ever found yourself stuck in a meeting or entangled in a company lunch at an all you can eat sushi buffet place where the dehydrated looking maguro reminds you of the worn out and red faced soccer mom you saw last Tuesday as she desperately tried to finish her grocery shopping and even though she was walking with a limp as she pushed the cart she didn't notice it was because she had a half smashed portabella mushroom stuck under her shoe and you think how life can try to trap you but you decide to not let it box you in so you reach into your pocket and from your secret stash you take a few plain M&Ms and quickly pop them in your mouth but as you begin to savor their crunchy sweetness you notice one of them is disturbingly chewy, which an M&M never should be, and the appalled expression arrives on your face just as you realize your boss is asking you how it's going so you decide to go big and you say "It's sucking right now" and he laughs and agrees and all that fortifies you enough to make it to 5:01?

Auto Pilot

In November I was in a daylong meeting with a group of co-workers. Luckily, we had some executives in the meeting who had set up a nice dinner at the end of the day. We just had to make it through the training sessions and motivational talks and then we would have a nice, relaxing dinner.

The final presentation of the day was about how our business needs to stay ahead of the competition. Vincent, our senior VP of sales, gave the talk. He used the 2008 Summer Olympics to illustrate why even the small things make a difference when going against top level competition. He focused on the Olympic swimming events. First he talked about how hard all the athletes train and prepare, their long hours in the pool and the weight room, their diets, and their sleep requirements. All of those elite swimmers live and breathe to realize their dream of winning at the Olympics. They were dedicated to that dream of winning.

Vincent talked about the fairness of the race environment. Everyone starts at the same time. Everyone swims straight ahead. Everyone swims in the same water at the same time. Everyone is drug tested, too. He asked us "Given the race conditions are so even and given how similar the athletes train, what is it that determines who wins? What gives one swimmer that winning edge?"

We gave the answers most people would give; winners have a greater will to win, they have more focus, more determination, they train harder. Vincent said all those mattered to some degree, but at the elite level everyone possesses all of those things. However, there was one 'small' factor showing up in *ninety-four percent* of the gold medal winners. More than 9 out of every 10 gold medal winners in the swimming events had this seemingly insignificant attribute.

Early in 2008, Speedo announced a new line of swimsuits. The LZR Racer was unveiled in February of that year. The suit reportedly would improve a swimmer's time by 1.9 to 2.2 percent. Michael Phelps, along with many other swimmers, adopted the LZR Racer. Many other swimmers did not make the switch. Those who did not adopt the Speedo probably thought "How much of a difference could a swimsuit make?"

When all the swimming events wrapped up, it was revealed that not only were 94% of all gold medalists wearing the LZR, but 89% of all medalists wore the Speedo LZR Racer. In addition, over 60 Olympic swimming records were set by those swimmers during the 2008 games.

Vincent reiterated that almost everything else was equal between the competitors. The most consistent difference between winners and losers was the type of swimsuit. On the surface, it would seem one competition-grade swimsuit would be pretty much like any other competition-grade suit, but clearly at the Olympic level of competition, a 1-2% improvement can be the difference between standing on the podium and standing on the sideline.

Vincent concluded his talk by drawing a parallel between those swimmers and our customers. "Most of our customers, like most of the Olympic swimmers, want the best product, the product that will give them a winning edge over their competition. If we can show our existing customers and our potential customers how they can win with us, we will continue to grow in market share and market value. Our job, us in this room right now, our job is to find that extra 2% in our products, our services and our support and then demonstrate that advantage to current and future customers. A simple improvement over the competition can be the difference between us making the sale and us watching the competition wave a signed contract in our faces. We win when we show customers they will win with us! At tonight's dinner, spend some time discussing your 2% ideas with each other. Okay, that's it! Go and enjoy your dinner! Have fun!"

With the final meeting done, the only remaining challenge was getting from our meeting location in Santa Clara to the restaurant 25 miles away in Palo Alto. For an evening commute, traffic congestion between those two cities can't be solved by Liquid Plummer or a 40 caliber machinegun. It's a pain to drive no matter how you approach it. Fortunately, we had a very capable organizer and she had chartered a bus. Everyone was to hop on the bus, go to dinner in Greyhound style, and then take the bus back to the meeting location. We would leave the driving to a professional so we could relax and talk on the way there and back.

Alas, due to a business call I got stuck at the meeting place and missed the bus so I had to make the drive on my own. When I got to Palo Alto there was no parking in front of the restaurant. I had to circle around the area to find a parking place. I finally found an open slot a couple blocks away from the place. It was on a residential street. My little car just fit into the open spot. When I got out of my car, I noticed most of the houses still had their Halloween decorations up, even though it was a good two weeks past the event. I saw ghosts, goblins, skeletons, a huge, old scary-faced jack-o-lantern and some full-size zombies.

After taking in the local scenery, I trucked on over to the dinner hangout, arriving about 20 minutes late. Everyone else already had a drink or a small plate of appetizers in hand. I just had my first sip of wine when it was time for us to sit down to dinner. I had a good dinner with co-workers, had another glass and a half of wine, told everyone we should focus our 2% effort on making our product the easiest to install and simplest to configure. Then I listened for the end. When the bus arrived it was time for us to go. Everyone else headed for the bus. I headed back to my little car.

Now let me ask you, have you ever been driving on auto-pilot and suddenly realized you were driving on auto-pilot ? Driving by habit, while your mind was on something else ? I was probably 4 miles down the road, headed home from the dinner, cruising along the highway and thinking about summer Olympics, gold medals, and swimsuits when I alerted myself to being on auto-pilot. Whenever this happened in the past, the first thing I did was check the rear-view mirror to make sure I didn't have a convoy of flashing police lights behind me.

It was no different this time. I snapped out of it and instantly looked to where the rear-view mirror should have been. The odd thing was the mirror wasn't there. Instead of a mirror, I was looking at a shiny, glistening orange wall. No mirror, just orange. "That's really weird" I tell myself. Then I quickly realize I better check the traffic ahead of me. Better make sure I'm not tailgating anyone. Uh-oh, most of the front windshield is not there! The same orange wall extends in both directions from the center point where the mirror should have been. This wall blocks most of the area where my front windshield should be. The only openings, the only places where I can see out of, are two isosceles triangles. One triangle is right in front of me and the other is way over to my right. Both are about 24 inches tall by 16 inches wide at the base. Neither have any windshield glass. They're just triangular openings in the wall.

This second oddity has heightened my awareness. Something is going on. That's when I notice a serious breeze blowing through my hair. While I'm continuing to peer out the triangle right in front of me, I wonder where the top level air flow is coming from since my car doesn't have a moon roof. I quickly glance straight up, just to check nothing weird has happened. My little car's bland beige roof is gone! It has been replaced by a scary openness. I take another glance. The crescent moon, twinkling stars and the night sky can see me right through the top of my car! I'm exposed to the heavens. But wait, the perimeter of this unexplained circular moon roof has the same orange glistening wall as the front of my car.

What the heck is going on? I start trying to take in the bigger picture, to see what other strangeness is around me. I try to look where the dashboard and steering wheel would be visible, but I can't get my vision to go that low. My vision is somehow stopped, as if it has hit the boundary of reality and can't go any lower. I can only see as low as the bottom of the two triangles.

When I try to look to my left or to my right, it's the same thing. I hit some boundary that blocks me from seeing anything beyond the orange area right in front of me and the moon roof area above me. I lift my left arm up off the steering wheel so I can at least see my own hand. I feel my grip loosen from the steering wheel that I can't see. I feel my arm rise up, and I wait to see it come into view. Nothing! I wave my whole arm right in front of my face. Still nothing. Even though I feel my arm moving, the only thing I see is what I've already been seeing, the orange wall, and through the two cut-out triangles the tail lights of freeway cars.

None of this makes sense. I concentrate and look harder, hoping I can discern something new. No arm, no hand. All I manage to notice is that the orange wall is fibrous, even a bit stringy. There are orange strands of various shades embedded in the wall. Some are as thick as spaghetti, while others are as thin as human hair. They crisscross each other in a random web-like pattern. I also notice the wall is bowed outward as it goes from one triangle to the other.

Taking a closer look at the where the triangles have been cut out, I can see the wall is about 6 inches thick and orange all the way through. As I re-examine the visible area, I wonder why I don't feel the same kind of breeze through the triangles as I do through the moon roof. Maybe it is because of where the triangles are positioned on the front curve. I'm not sure. I figure it must be some kind of physics thing that I don't really understand.

I hear motorcycles and through the triangle in front of me, I soon see two Harleys, with riders wearing black leather and skid lids, zoom past me. I say they have black leather because that's what Harley guys always wear, but, in fact, there's a darkness surrounding them that makes it impossible for me to be sure what they are wearing. The ambient light of the freeway traffic doesn't reveal anything save for a faint shine on the near side of their chrome skid lids.

When they are five yards in front of me, the riders simultaneously turn and look back at me. In the cool evening darkness no part of their flesh is exposed, but the facial bones painted on their skull masks are just visible. The masks give the riders an eerie bones-only look that takes on a more frightening, even hellish, look when brake lights from the car one lane over light up. Their skid lids take on a crimson glow and the bones turn a burnt orange. The devil's helpers would look like that, I think to myself.

As they stare at me, their stoic expressions reveal nothing of their thoughts or intentions. After a heart beat or two, the car driver lets off the brake and the redness is gone. The riders turn back around and accelerate down the road. I begin to breathe again.

That was creepy. They looked completely fleshless, but very capable of harm. Conversely I can feel all of my body, I can feel the goose bumps on my forearms and the tension in my feet, but I can't see any of me. My skin is sensitive to my surroundings, yet invisible to me. The riders quickly rode on and now I'm not so sure they existed, even though I saw them. I know I exist but I can't see any of myself.

My right knee is cold. I put my left hand back on the invisible steering wheel, taking hold of it at the twelve o'clock position. I take my right hand off the wheel and begin rubbing my knee to warm it up. As I do that, I can tell there is another breeze coming into the car and it is directed at my knee. After my knee is warmed up, I decide to find the source of the breeze so I reach forward. I can't see what my hand is touching, but it has to be the orange wall. It is both slimey and sticky to the touch. As I explore around, I find the opening where the wind is coming in. With my hand I trace around the opening. I discover it is another isosceles triangle. It feels like it is just a bit smaller than the other two. It is centered between the two top triangles, and a bit lower on the wall. The wind coming in is as cool as the night air, but given I'm driving along at freeway speed, the velocity of the wind is much lower than I would expect. It's actually a good thing because it would be much colder if the wind came blasting in at the expected rate. Why air comes through this one, but not the top two is one more mystery I file away.

In the process of exploring the lower triangle, I've managed to lean over to my right. My exploring is complete now and given that I can only see out of the top two triangles, I decide I better sit up straight so I can have the best view forward. After all, whatever else is happening, I am still driving on the freeway. In order to upright myself I use my right hand to push off from the bottom lip of the lower triangle, but after I start to push, my hand succumbs to the slipperiness of the mysterious interior decoration. The initial push gets my momentum going in the desired directions. I start to straighten up, but when my hand slips off the triangle's lip I lose my balance, unexpectedly falling back to the right. With the sudden loss of balance, my left foot automatically kicks up and forward as a counter balance.

It's an involuntary, uncontrolled kick. My foot quickly flies forward until it sinks into a mushy resistance. My foot has enough force that it pushes into the thick substance until the front half of my shoe must be buried in the stuff. There's a splaah sound as my shoe penetrates what surely must be the continuation of the orange wall. Great, now I'm going to have one and a half shoes looking neat and clean, as is my usual attire, and one half of one shoe looking like it was attacked by a pack of rabid carrots.

The good thing is that with my foot being stuck in the wall, it anchors my balance and I'm able to first stop my fall and then straighten myself back into an upright sitting position.

I'm relieved to be back in the normal driving position, but my right hand feels slimey and my left foot is planted in the front wall. My hand problem I easily solve by wiping the goo onto my pants leg. Of course I can't see my hand or my pants leg, but my palm feels much cleaner. I return my right hand to the invisible steering wheel.

Now I'm on to freeing my left foot. I continue to keep my vehicle in my lane and at a speed that blends in with my fellow travelers. I begin wiggling my foot with the expectation that I'll need to work it back and forth in order to loosen the gooey grip that holds it in place. To my surprise, during the initial wiggle my foot starts to slid over to the right. It's like my foot, even though it is stuck in the wall, is doing a crab walk to the right. As it moves to the right, the grip loosens and I can easily pull my foot free and set it back on the floor.

My foot is free, but the way it became free is odd. I want to understand what happened so I decide to do some methodical exploring down there. I cautiously slide my left foot forward along the floor until my toes hits the front wall. Then I slide my foot to the left, thinking my foot will end up in the corner where the side of the vehicle meets the front wall, but there is no corner. With my toes against the front wall, my foot slides in an arc as it moves to the left. Just as the orange wall in front of me has a curve to it, so does the wall that meets the floor.

My plan was to explore the front wall, starting on left edge and then moving to the right. Since there is no left edge I just begin exploring the front wall about where I expected to find the edge. I begin by slowing moving my toes up, then down, the wall, feeling for something unusual, some kind of break or bump in the surface. There's nothing unusual on the first pass. I move my foot to the right and make another up and down pass. On this next up pass, my toes catch on a crack near the top of their motion. I proceed to use the front of my shoe to investigate this break in the wall. I make a futile attempt to glance down there, but my vision is still restricted.

With my shoe I probe the area around the crack. I can tell the crack gets larger as it moves to the right. I even find the wall wound where my shoe punched it. To the right of the wound the crack continues to widen and that explains why my shoe came loose the way it did.

The bottom lip of the crack is a smooth arc that continues beyond what I can reach with my foot. The top lip of the crack is a smooth arc, too, but it is a tighter arc. I can't feel all of the opening because it extends too far to the right, but what I've felt makes me think something like a crescent moon shape has been cut out of the vehicle.

I move my left foot back to the floorboard. Now I'm in the most common of driving positions, hands on steering wheel, right foot on gas, left foot on floorboard, vision directed straight ahead, but everything else around me is odd. As I continue homeward I take stock of my situation. The vehicle is some sticky, stringy, slippery orange thing. There is a round opening in the roof, two large triangles cut out of the wall at eye level, a smaller triangle centered and below the other triangles and below the triangles is a crescent-like opening that spans most of the front of the vehicle.

I am a rational and logical man but the evidence before me leads me to a logical conclusion that is not at all rational. Given my situation there is only one answer. I must be driving a pumpkin, well, not just a pumpkin, but a giant jack-o-lantern...on the freeway, no less. The slippery, slimy orange interior, the classic three-triangle-and-a-mouth jack-o-lantern carvings and the open top all give evidence to this obvious, but crazy conclusion. I'm traveling 65mph on the 101 freeway inside a big-ass pumpkin.

Luckily, I'm in the San Francisco Bay Area so it is unlikely anyone is going to bother me or my jumbo pumpkin vehicle. So long as I don't go too slow or cut in front of some other fruit on the road I should be fine. By the time I've worked all this out I am two thirds of the way home. I figure just go with it. I keep on pumpkining home.

I'm about a mile from my freeway exit and I need to move over to the slow lane. The one triangle in front of me doesn't give me a lot of side to side visibility and the other cutout is at too sharp of an angle for me to see anything out of it. Added to that, there are no mirrors. With my field of vision restricted, all I can do is hope the lane is clear. I automatically reach for the turn signaler. Seeing as I'm driving a pumpkin, I am surprised when my hand actually finds the lever. I lift the lever up to indicate I'm moving over to my right. I don't hear any blinker sound, but then I remember that other than the biker's noise, it has been a silent ride home anyway. After a brief, hopeful pause, I slowly navigate into the right lane. I breathe a sigh of relief once I'm safely into the lane.

I make it off the freeway and onto the city street without any problem. My good fortune continues as all 7 traffic lights home are green or yellow for me. I don't remember that ever happening before.

The pumpkin gets me to my neighborhood safely and soundly, but with all my moving around inside it, I feel I've picked up my own coat of slipperiness. As I park the pumpkin in my driveway, I wonder just how slippery my shoes will be and will I be able to make it up the driveway's modest incline. I contemplate this as I move the pumpkin-vehicle's shifter into park.

Now, I'm sure it didn't happen this way, but there seemed to be only a blink of my eyes between the time I put the pumpkin into park and the time I'm walking across my living room, headed straight for my bedroom and my bed. How I got from the pumpkin to the living room is a mystery to me.

I suddenly feel so tired I don't even have the strength to flick on the living room's overhead light. This is my house and I'm sure I can navigate my way from the living room to my bedroom with just the normal soft glow from the hallway night light.

I make it okay to my bedroom entrance, but as I turn from the hallway into my room, I trip on something that's out of place, maybe one of my old running shoes my puppy left in the doorway. Whatever it is, it catches me by surprise. I feel myself stumble forward and start to fall towards the foot of my bed. In my weariness, I can't keep my balance. I'm bent at the waist, with my head and shoulders way too far forward and my arms out in front of me. It feels like I'm getting ready to dive into a swimming pool. Since my bed is my goal away, I go ahead and jump-dive towards it. It's a short jump.

As I splash down onto my bed, something unexpected happens. I don't land on top of my bed cover. I pass right through it, like a swimmer passes through the pool's surface when he launches himself from the starting platform. I'm quickly submerged below the bed cover and I'm sliding between the sheets at what feels like an incredibly fast speed. I wonder "Am I wearing a LZR?" My arms are still stretched out in front of me while I'm looking straight down, at my white fitted sheet. I can tell I'm sliding because I feel the top and bottom sheets moving down my body, from my back to my bottom to my legs and from my chest to my abdomen to my knees and feet. I see orange streaks, like pumpkin-colored raindrops on a window, pass through my vision. Must be fibers coming off my outstretched hands and arms.

My sliding goes on and on until I feel a strain in my chest. I realize I'm holding my breath. I begin to breathe quickly. My slippery speed immediately slows down and continues to slow down as my breathing slows. I get my breathing under control and at the same time I gracefully lower my arms. Using a broad, arching stroke, I pull them from their straight ahead diving position to where they are close to my torso. In a swimmer's world, this big motion would be the working portion of a butterfly stroke. It would propel the swimmer forward, but it has the opposite effect on me. I've slowed to a lazy, drifting pace as my arms come to rest against my side. Never the less, it feels to me like I've been swimming for 25 meters in the whitest of water. I continue to slow down. Then something I already knew hits me, I'm in my bed.

I sense I'm about to reach my pillow at the headboard. I know I can't go to sleep on my belly. I've got to flip onto my back. While I've still got a little momentum, I flip myself over. I'm on my back and I feel my head slide up onto my comforting pillow just as I come to a stop. In spite of all this night's strangeness, with the covers now keeping me snug and warm, I feel safe, warm and relaxed.

I know I'm already asleep, so I open my eyes just to check. Yep, I'm just where I'm supposed to be. I slip off to dreamland and have a good night's sleep.

Foul Air Repellent Team

Chapter 1

All of the high tech companies I have worked at had cubicles for most, and sometimes all, of their workers. They typically had the cubes with the waist high walls, not the taller walled cubicles. With those short walls, everyone could see everyone else, whether sitting at their desk or walking around. The shorter walls saved money for the company, and it also made communication between workers a lot easier. Good communication is incredibly important at high tech companies.

Those companies that had a few walled offices usually assigned them to executives, people in sales, and folks in HR. That makes sense because they often have to engage in confidential conversations. One of the startup companies I worked at had just a few walled offices, so the CEO had one, the two sales guys shared one, and the HR lady had the other one. The company had just one conference room.

When I went there for the initial interview, I talked with some of the engineers. That session took place in a few of the engineer's cubicles and in the one conference room. It went well enough that I got called back for a second round of interviews. I passed the second round and a few weeks later I started at the new place.

My first day schedule was to meet with Tom, my new manager, at 10:30, then go around and meet the rest of the engineering team, then go to lunch with the whole group. After lunch I'd meet with the HR lady and she would go over the employment and benefit forms.

The morning went smooth, as did most of the lunch. For lunch we went to the Indian buffet just around the corner. I was about half way through my second plate of chana masala, veggie beryani, garlic nan and lamb korma, when Cliff, the senior engineer, asked me if I'd met the HR lady already. I said no, I'd only met the receptionist, but I'd meet Marcia, the HR lady, after lunch.

He, along with a couple other guys, let out easy laughs.

"What's funny?" I asked.

"There are two things you need to know about Marcia. First, her clothes are expensive, but never seem to fit her. She's always tugging and adjusting and covering up, as if something's going to fall out or be exposed. You'd think a woman in her 40s could buy clothes that fit. Anyway, you just have to accept that."

"Okay"

"Second, she goes a bit heavy on the perfume so you'll probably want to breathe really shallow when you meet with her."

"Oh man, how bad is it?" I asked.

"Just be glad she has her own office. Although...it's really a double-edged sword. Her office keeps the perfume from spreading across the whole company, but if you are trapped in there with her, it can be tough."

Before we can continue this conversation, my boss interrupts by tapping his water glass and then he makes the obligatory welcome speech. I follow him with my "Great to be here" speech. After that, the conversation turns to work stuff and what I'll be working on. We don't get back to perfumed Marica.

When we get back from lunch my boss walks me to Marcia's office. Of course I remember Cliff's warning so as we walk there I'm secretly taking deeper and deeper breaths, thinking maybe I can hold my breath and sign all the forms really fast and get out of there before I have to inhale.

My boss introduces us. Marcia is sitting at her desk and as she stands up, I step into her office and reach across her desk to shake her hand. As I say "Nice to meet you, Marcia" all my deep breathing investment evaporates simply because speaking carries it away. Now I have nothing in the air bank.

"Come on in and close the door" Marcia says as she sits back down at her desk.

Tom has headed back to his cube, but as I start to close Marcia's door I act like he just called me. I stick my head out the door as if to hear him. "What was that, Tom ?" I say, to make the illusion more realistic, then I slip in one more desperate, deep inhale of unadorned air, fearing the unsmelt. I close the door and sit down. I clench my teeth, thinking that'll somehow keep bad air out.

Before we even start to talk, Marcia's phone rings and she answers it. It sounds like a recruiter. They proceed to have a short, eight minute conversation. All the while, Marcia fidgets in her chair, adjusting her skirt, pulling her buttonless jacket tighter only to have it go right back to where it was, fixing hidden shoulder straps and checking her necklace isn't twisted.

Less than a minute into all of this, I'm struggling to hold my breath. It feels like I'm half way through a heart attack. As my heart is banging louder and louder against my chest, I decide dying on the first day of the job is not a good start, especially since I haven't signed any forms just yet.

I convince myself I can take it, after all, I've ridden in lots of perfumed stuffed elevators in Laughlin, Reno and Vegas. How bad can her perfume be, I ask myself.

I let out a little spent air. I take in a little office air. Nothing bad so far. Marcia continues her phone conversation, unaware of my reluctance. I let out a little more air and take in a bit more. There's something there.

I don't know perfumes or colognes by name. I know good and bad. I know pleasant and unpleasant. This something is slightly unpleasant. Not rotten eggs, not skunky roadkill, but slightly unappealing, more like a sweaty t-shirt over in the corner of the room.

I decide to relax a bit and take a few normal breathes. Marcia continues to chat away with the recruiter. She stops fidgeting long enough to slide a folder across her desk towards me. She opens the folder, points at the forms within it and mouths "Take a look". I read through stuff as she talks with the recruiter.

When she finishes with the recruiter, I've skimmed through most of the forms. We talk some, I ask some questions and she answers them. It's cordial, with a minor nuisance of bad perfume. We end the meeting with Marcia asking me to return the completed forms by the end of the week.

It wasn't nearly as bad as Cliff had suggested at lunch.

Later that day, I'm in the men's room, washing up, when Cliff walks in. He starts up a conversation.

"Were you in a frat at college?" he asks.

Given his earlier warning about Marcia, I was expecting a question about my meeting with her, but I'm not so surprised I can't answer his question. "No, no frat for me"

"How about the military ? Any time in the Army, Navy, Air Force or Marines?"

I shake my head 'no'.

"Have you joined any clubs or organized groups ?" he asks.

"Just the Boy Scouts. Why do you ask?"

Ignoring my question, Cliff says "Ahh, yes. The Scouts. What did you have to do to join?"

"Hmmm... Just learn the pledge, I think."

"We are a small company here. We have only one club that I'm aware of and I think you should join it."

I'm not sure where this is going so I take a step towards the bathroom exit and then reply "I'm not much of a joiner, Cliff."

"Fair enough" Cliff says, then he continues " but let me explain. There are eight of us and we call ourselves the Foul Air Repellant Team. Our mission is to fight and defeat the excessive use of perfumes, colognes and body sprays in our workplace environment."

"So who besides Marcia qualifies..."

"Just Marcia"

"So your club's mission is to get Marcia to reduce her use of perfume?'

"Yep. That's it."

The bathroom door is within my reach and this conversation is taking a strange turn. I'd like to just get back to my desk, but Cliff is the senior engineer. He's not technically my boss but I don't want to be rude to him so I ask.

"How do you go about that ?"

"We once tried the direct line and simply asked her to skip the perfume or at least reduce it, but to no avail. She promised to go lighter, but none of us noticed a difference so now we fight a stealth battle. We fight fire with fire."

"That doesn't make sense. You fight her perfume with your own perfume?" I ask.

"Yes, our own perfume" Cliff makes finger quotes as he says perfume, then he continues "We conveniently deliver our perfurme" finger quotes again " to her walled office while she is in some meeting or visiting the restroom"

There's a pause while I think about what he means by "perfume". I decide to be direct. "It sounds like you go fart in her office when she's not there."

"Yes" Cliff replies. Then he raises his right index finger, leans forward and says " but very diligently and very discretely."

"Diligently and discretely? " I question.

"Diligently is easy since there are eight of us. We can easily keep track of where she goes and when she is headed back to her office. We use hand signals and Yahoo IM to set things up and deploy our messenger. With eight of us, someone is bound to have a good one on deck, but we don't just go willy-nilly stinking it up as soon as she leaves. We carefully, discretely deliver our response just a few seconds before she returns to her office." Cliff replies pridefully.

"Aaaah. That explains the big fan in her office." I reply. "But how come I didn't notice the fragrance of battle when I met her after lunch?"

"We try not to take out innocent bystanders." he replies.

"Wow. That's very considerate of you. So it's only when she will be there by herself?"

"Yes."

I've heard enough and finally grab the door handle, but before I leave I say "I have to tell you Cliff, I didn't find her perfume all that bad. I'm not sure she is deserving of this."

"Fair enough" Cliff says "Take some time to decide. Maybe when you return your health care forms to her it will change your mind." With that Cliff steps into a stall and I head back to my cube.

The next few days I spend reading product docs, reviewing code and talking with other engineers about the next release of our product. The only time I see Marcia is when she is talking with Tom or one of the other managers.

My cube faces the main walkway to the breakroom and restrooms, but I'm three rows back from it and I don't smell anything from her or anyone else as they go back and forth along the walkway. On the other hand, Cliff's cube is right on the far side of the walkway. He practically has to notice anyone that goes either way.

A couple times after Marcia walked along the hallway, I'd glance at Cliff. He always had his head down, as if reading something on his desk or he'd be facing his computer screen, but either way he would have a hand over his nose. He never made eye contact with me, but I strongly suspect he knew I was looking.

On Thursday of my first week, I'm eating my sandwich and chips in the breakroom. Pat, our young receptionist, walks in and we exchange 'hi's. I go back to my lunch while she gets a container out of the refrig and pops it into the microwave. There's only one table in the breakroom so when her meal is heated, she asks "Can I join you?". She is cute so of course I think 'yes' and 'no' at the same time, but answer "Sure".

We make small talk. She asks where I worked before. I ask how long she has worked at the company and how she got the job. I tell her my only complaint so far is that the benefits are not as good as what I had at my last place.

She says "Speaking of benefits, Cliff said he already talked with you about joining our team."

"Team?" I reply.

"You know, the Foul Air Repellant Team. I love that name." she says with a smile.

The break room has a door, closed right now, so I don't worry too much about someone overhearing us.

"I told Cliff I didn't think Marcia deserves that treatment."

"Oh? Have you smelled her today? When she walked through the lobby this morning I swear even the fish in the aquarium held their noses."

"I did notice her perfume back on Monday. It was unpleasant, but not overpowering."

"Try it today...it will change your mind. Do you still have forms to give her?"

"Yes."

"Return them to her today. Please."

"I was going to anyway. I was just waiting to catch her in her office."

The break room door opens and Tom walks in. Everyone says 'hi' to each other.

I'm done with my lunch and get up to leave. Pat says "I'll buzz you when she gets back from lunch, okay?"

I just shrug and walk out. I take a walk around the block before going back to my desk.

At about 1:20 my desk phone rings. It's Pat telling me Marcia has just returned from lunch and is in her office now. I grab all my completed forms and head to her office. The door is open. Marcia is reading something on her computer while chewing on her necklace. I tap on the door frame. She looks up, takes the necklace out of her mouth and says "Hi William"

"Hi, can I drop these with you now?"

"Sure, come on in. Have a seat while I look them over."

I sit down, and start breathing shallow and a bit quicker than normal. I hand her the forms.

Marcia is quickly flipping through the pages. She pauses on a page. "You forgot to initial here for automatic deposit" she says. She sets the form on her desk midway between us and she leans toward me so she can point at the spot on the form. I move in to get a closer look.

Chapter 2

Remember your first over-the-age-of-21 summer trip to Las Vegas? It was a nice day in the casino. It was a comfortable 70 something, without the worry of sunburn or the concern for wind-dried skin and no desert sun glaring down at you. The breakfast buffet was jumbo good and with the table games, the slots, and the sports bars, there was plenty going on inside the pleasant, friendly casino, but for some reason you decided it would be nice to get some fresh air and see a bit more of the strip, maybe go see the volcano. It was about 10:40 AM.

With your first step outside, as the casino door slips from your instantly sweaty fingertips, you realize you have magically crossed over into a different world. It's not just a little warmer and a tad brighter than inside the casino. No. You've stepped into a world that is irrationally hot and ridiculously bright. Sweat begins gushing from your arm pits as if they held hidden water balloons that suddenly bursts open. The brightness has you squinting so hard you see your own eye brow hairs.

These two worlds are so different from each other you refused to accept they existed right next to each other until you experienced them side-by-side yourself. Now you've made a cross over to a world your friends warned you about, but you didn't believe existed. You had to experience the irrational, unexplainable world to be convinced it existed. The door is right there and, oh yeah, the volcano will look much better at night, anyway. Back inside you go.

As I move in to look at where Marcia is pointing, I make a similar cross over. There is no door for me to walk through, but from one breath to the next I pass from the common comfort of office space atmosphere into a sweltering stench so strong it seems impossible it could be invisible. I'm so shocked by it that I gasp, or more accurately, I do a half gasp because I quickly realize inhaling is inviting this vileness deeper into me. My brain starts shouting all kinds of orders, like a submarine captain trying to avoid any more depth charge damages. I try to shutdown my whole pulmonary system. All full stop. Paused silence.

Stunned as I am I know I don't want to just float there so I take the pen that Marcia is offering me, quickly scribble my initials on the form and exhale as I fall back into my chair. The whole episode was two, maybe three, seconds but that was enough. I've crossed back over. I'm safely back in my chair and normal office air. I'm immediately ready to flee. I start to get up, but Marcia, back in her chair, says "Let me make you copies" so I put my left hand over my nose , pinching it 95% closed, and wait while she uses her copy machine that's behind her desk. It seems safe in my chair right now, but I feel like there is another stealth stink attack just waiting to happen.

The copy machine finishes, I stand up and step towards the office door. I am facing towards the hallway, away from Marcia. I'm posed there, still pinching my nose with my left hand and with my right hand, reaching back behind me for my copies. I know it looks awkward, like a relay runner reaching back for the baton, but I'm not up for another nasal assault. Marcia sees me and asks "In a hurry?" As I nod yes, she rolls up my copies and slaps then into my extended, open hand. I sprint out of her office and in to open air safety.

I drop off my copies at my desk, then head to the restroom to wash my face. As I pass by Cliff's desk I nod for him to follow me. He does.

No one else is in the bathroom so we talk, but first I have to splash cold water on my face. I leave some of it there as I say

"Okay, so I'm in."

"I knew you'd see the light." Cliff replies. After a pause, he continues "There's only one thing you've got to do. Like every other club, we have an initiation process. Once you hear about it, I'm sure you'll agree that ours is a simple...and even natural initiation."

Cliff tells me what I need to do to become a member. I agree to it and we set the next day as the initiation day. That night I eat a healthy dinner and get a good night's sleep.

I get into work about 9:15 the next day, Friday. Cliff doesn't show up until 9:45. He sends me a Yahoo IM saying the initiation will have to wait until the afternoon, probably between 2:30 and 3:00. I reply okay, but wonder to myself if I'm up to the task. The rest of the morning and early afternoon I'm not getting much work done. I keep re-

reading the same four pages of product documentation over and over while I try not to think about my impending initiation.

Just after 2:00 Cliff stops by my desk and tells me I will get a 'go' IM from either him or Pat. That will put the process in motion. Cliff tells me I will have about 10 seconds to complete my initiation task.

At 2:33 a 'go' from Pat pops up on my Yahoo messenger and I move into action. As I stand up I look towards Cliff's desk. He's not there. The clock is ticking so I've got to keep going anyway. At the main walkway I make a right turn and head towards Marcia's office. When I get to her doorway I realize I've forgotten the manila folder I'm supposed to carry as my cover. It's too late now for me to go back and get it. I step into her office and quietly close the door most of the way shut. I step to her side of the desk and successfully, abundantly complete the initiation requirement. I'm now a proud member of the Foul Air Repellent Team.

As I open the door and start to walk out of Marcia's office, the CEO walks by. He sees my new face and steps into the doorway. He's blocking me from getting out of Marcia's office and worse yet, he's put himself on the fringe of the battle zone.

"Hey, William, welcome aboard." he says enthusiastically as he extends his right hand towards me. As I put my hand out, I sense that what I've left deeper in the office is expanding and is now creeping past me, towards the CEO. As our hands meet, I see his smile falter a bit and then recover.

As we shake hands I feel compelled to explain myself but I don't have much to offer. "Hi Donny, I was just..aaah" I verbally stumble .

Just then, Marcia steps into view. "Hey, what are you guys doing in my doorway?" she says as she squeezes past us and moves to the chair behind her desk.

"Oh, gawd" she exclaims. "Which one of you did that?" she demands as she pushes the 'Hi' button on her big fan and then gives each of us a hard stare. There's three seconds of silence, except for the sound of the oscillating fan and the rustle of mini-blinds.

"Not me" says the CEO as he takes a step back from Marcia's office.

More silence as Marcia stares at me while adjusting her skirt's waistband and then checking both her ear rings.

"Why, William ? Why would you do this?"

I'm completely embarrassed and without words. I know my face can't possibly be as red as it feels, but I'm sure it is close.

Marcia continues "Who put you up to this ?"

"I..."

Marcia breaks eye contact with me to look at the CEO. "Donny, I know this is some childish engineer thing. Can you talk to them?"

"Yes, yes. I'll send out an email tomorrow."

"That's useless. You have to talk to them face to face."

As Marcia is talking I see she is looking at something moving behind Donny. "Cliff. Cliff!" she calls.

Cliff waves to us from the hallway outside Marcia's office. Marcia motions for him to come inside and join us. Cliff shakes his head no and then motions for all of us to step outside and join him.

Once we are in the hallway, Marica says to our CEO "Now's a good time to start and Cliff is a good person to start with."

Donny nods, then starts "Cliff, I don't know if you do this or if you know who does it, but I'm asking you, as senior engineer, tell all the programmers to please leave Marcia's office alone. Take it to the bathroom, take it outside but no more of this fouling in her office."

Before Cliff says anything, Marcia jumps in. "You know, I can't even get plants to survive in there. They wilt, literally wilt. They eventually look like they've been suffocated to death. It's that bad!"

"I don't know what you guys are talking about" Cliff says, but there's a lack of honesty in his voice and demeanor.

"Right" Marcia replies, then reaches inside her blouse and adjusts her left shoulder pad.

"Well?" she asks of Cliff.

"Okay. " Cliff says. "I *think* I know who's doing this and I'll talk to them. I *might* be able to get them to stop or at least curtain their offensives, but I just want you to know" and at this point he looks at Donny "it wasn't an engineer that started these bombing raids."

Marcia, Cliff and I look at Donny. He's looking at Marcia and she says "Donny, what does he mean by that?"

Donny takes his hands out of his CEO Dockers and throws them palms up as he explains "Okay...It was one time and it was an emergency." He pleads. Then he continues, "The bathroom was closed for cleaning and we had venture capitalists already in the lobby. I couldn't use the restroom and I couldn't get passed the vc guys to go outside, the conference room was in use, the sales guys were on their phones" his voice is getting higher and a tinge of desperation creeps in. "There was no place available but your office...and with all the perfume you wear, I figured you wouldn't even notice."

"And what about your own office?" Marcia asks.

"Are you kidding me? The vc guys were joining me in there in less than a minute. I wasn't going to have them walk into a mess like that. Your office was my only hope."

Marcia shakes her head in disbelief. "Unbelievable. I guess that explains one time." Marcia turns to Cliff and asks "How did it become this running joke ?"

Cliff must have expected that question. "I can answer that" he says matter-of-factly. "As you may remember, I had joined the company earlier that same week. I happened to be returning my forms to you when I saw... and heard Donny in your office. "

Mentally, I'm starting to step away from all these people. This topic, this conversation, is too much like what I hear when I go camping with my uncles. They get slightly drunk while sitting around the evening camp fire and eventually the "conversation" turns to a competition of body noises.

Cliff continues, "I had already noticed how much perfume you wear. I even mentioned it to you."

"Wait a minute" Marcia demands. "I didn't even start to wear perfume until my office had been mysteriously bombarded at least three different times. My perfume was a response to your nonsense."

"Oh no" says Cliff, "I remember the first time I walked into your office I smelled something bad, something offensive. Your perfume ..."

It's time for me to jump in and be the hero. "Wait a minute! Let's not argue and fight over which came first. It's a chicken and egg thing that can't be solved." Everyone is giving me looks of confusion, but it shows they are listening so I continue. "The important thing is that we *all* stop. We work together ...so let's work together" Looking at Marcia, I say "You didn't always wear perfume to work, right? Can you agree to no more perfume if they stop? If they stay out of your office ?" She looks from me to Cliff to me, then gives a reluctant nod. I look to Cliff and say "No more perfume, okay?" I use the finger quotes around perfume.

"I'm sure if Marcia stops wearing her perfume I can get agreement from the team, too" Cliff says.

"Team?" Marcia asks.

I jump in with "Nevermind that. We agree to knock this stuff off. Right?"

"Yes! I agree with William. Everyone stop" says Donny. Marcia and Cliff eventually agree, too.

As Cliff and I walk towards our cubes, he says "Man, this place is going to be so boring now"

The next Monday I drop by Marcia's. She's on the phone, but she sees me at the door and waves me in. "Just a sec" she says to her caller and then looks at me. While she is looking at me, I take a deep breath, inhale, exhale, then say "It's good to be here. That's all." She smiles and replies "Thank you, William. And I agree"

On my walk back to my desk I think "This is a good place to work. The company has potential, the people are smart and hard working and in a small way I have helped make it a friendlier place to work." I am feeling good about myself as I take my desk seat. Soon as I sit down I hear this loud "phhhhht" coming from right under me. There are roars of laughter all around me as I quickly jump up, turn around and find a deflated whoopee cushion on my chair. "What the hell?" I say with some anger. There's more laughter.

Cliff, Tom, the other engineers, Marcia, Donny and even the sales guys are all laughing it up. I've been setup. I pick up the whoopee cushion like it really is stinky. I know Cliff must have done this so I turn to him and say "I knew it was there. I saw it all along."

Cliff is laughing too much to reply. My immediate anger has faded already, but I have to try to defend myself. I turn to Marcia "I *knew* it was there. I just played along." A smile slips across my face as I hear my own foolish assertion.

"Sure, William, sure you did" she says. She turns back to her office. Everyone else turns back to their work, too.

No one is listening, but as I sit down to work, I set the cushion on my desk, and with a chuckle I say "This is a good place to work".

Dawn Shark Date

By the time Jesse was 17 his family had moved five times. He was born in Texas and spent his first seven years there. Then his dad moved the family to Louisiana for 16 months. Jesse's sister, Alice, was born in Alaska, where the Colton's lived for four years. They spent three years in China and then 8 months in Saudi Arabia. The latest move was, in Jesse's opinion, a good move. After four and half years in foreign countries the Colton family was headed back to the States.

In August Jesse's dad had signed a two year consulting contract with an oil drilling company located in Bakersfield, California. To Jesse, that meant he would get to spend his junior and senior years of high school back in America. American food, American tv, American sports, American girls and everything else America had to offer was waiting for him.

The last four school years Jesse and Alice were home schooled by their mom. In fact, Alice had never been to a regular school and her only impression of classroom life was from reading Harry Potter with her mom, along with vague recollections of what her brother would say when he got home from school in Alaska. Alice was hopeful and excited about going to a real school. She asked her mom a million questions

"Mom, will I get to ride a train like Harry?"
"Will I get my own books?"
"Do I have to live at school?"
"Can I get a lunch box? One with Harry?"
"Will I have new friends?"

Jesse was anxious, too. He wanted to get to Bakersfield before school got started. He knew as a new kid he would stick out much more if he joined a new school that had already started the school year than if he were new at the very beginning of school year. He figured if they moved soon enough he might have a few friends by the time school started.

Unfortunately, at the last minute the Saudi oil company asked Jesse's dad to stay an extra six weeks to help implement more of his efficiency recommendations. The Saudi company offered Mr. Colton twice his normal consulting rate to stay. He took the offer once he made sure the Bakersfield company was okay with pushing his start date back. The family didn't leave for California until late September. By the time they got settled in Bakersfield it was October.

Jesse started at Dawson High School on Monday, the 3rd of October. It would turn out to be the second most memorable day of his whole K-12 experience. His most memorable experience took place at Folger elementary, in Juneau Alaska, where he attended class from second to fifth grade.

When taking recess outside, every Alaskan elementary kid wore some type of head cover; a beanie or a touk or a cap with ear flaps, along with a jacket, usually the puffy, down filled ones, and mittens.

The puffier your jacket, the more likely you were to get punched at recess. There were always three bullies, always 6th graders. They would make the rounds together at recess, stopping at the various play areas and picking out the couple kids with the puffiest or newest jackets.

Regardless of the bully or his victim, the conversation went essentially the same once the unlucky kid was identified. It consisted of three parts. The bully asked an introductory question, then asked the setup question, then delivered the punch line.

The Bully's friendly introduction; "Hey kid, nice jacket. Is it new?" or "Hey kid, nice jacket. Is it warm?" Naïve kids would initially welcome the attention and would give some polite reply like "Sure is". The more aware kids, typically sensing malice, would either just give a wary nod yes or a tepid "uh-huh".

The Bully's setup; While staring the kid down, "It's missing something. Know what it's missing?" or, even meaner, the bully would circle around the poor kid while saying "It seems to be missing something. Know what it is?" The two other bullies would give off smirks. This time the kid would give an almost imperceptible 'no' shake of his head. Experienced victims may have already started to leak tears and snot at this point.

The Bully's punchline; "I'll tell you what it's missing. It's missing the Alaska state motto, 'North to the future'". Delivered with the state motto was a slug to the victim's shoulder or chest. 'North' is when the punch arrived.

Jesse's first 'Punch to the future' experience, as it was known amongst the kids, was when he was in third grade. Richie, his friend, and classmate, had a brother in fifth grade. Bobby, Richie's brother, had the misfortune of getting a puffy new jacket and mittens for Christmas.

That first week of school right after Christmas break was a busy time for the bullies. With so many new jacket victims to punch, they had to be careful not to get sore knuckles or sprained wrists from overuse. Bobby got his punch during the 10:15AM recess on Tuesday. Richie and Jesse watched it.

Besides dividing the kids up by grade, the school also divided them at recess by two larger groups. All kids had recess at the same time, but the 1st through 3rd graders had recess on one side of the school yard, while the 4th through 6th graders had the other side. A chain-linked fence was the divider.

Jesse had no older brother so he was completely unaware of the bully work that happened on the other side of the fence. His friend Richie knew what his brother had waiting for him. When Richie saw the bullies walking towards the tetherball poles where Bobby was playing, he figured it was his brother's time. As Richie started running to the divider fence, he called Jesse to follow him. "Come on, Jesse. Bobby's in for trouble!" They got to the fence in time to see Bobby lose his tetherball game and turn to leave. The three bullies were right there.

Wanting to get closer to his brother, Richie had his mittens and chin pushing on the chain links. He and Jesse were not near enough to hear what was being said at the poles, but Jesse heard Richie whisper "He's in for it now" as they watched the biggest bully walk around Bobby. When the big kid stopped, his back was towards Richie and Jesse. Bobby was mostly blocked from view by the sixth grader. There was a pause, then Jesse saw the big kid's shoulder jump toward Bobby. Bobby quickly bent over at the waist. As the big kid moved away, Jesse and Richie could see Bobby doubled over, holding the left side of his chest and letting his left arm hang limp.

Jesse had never sensed imminent danger until he heard it in his friend's voice. He hadn't been exposed to personal violence until he saw the bully walk away, leaving Bobby bent over in pain. Jesse's parents were respectful and mild-mannered people. They didn't argue or fight with each other or anyone else. They didn't let their kids watch violent shows or play violent games. Jesse had lived in a peaceful, happy world until that recess.

More than seeing Bobby bent over, the greater shock to Jesse was the bully's unprovoked attack and then seeing him calmly walk away after perpetrating such a violent act. Jesse would forever remember the whole scene, including the final image of Bobby rubbing his punched chest along with Richie saying "Yep, he got it" and then letting out a small cry and a couple sniffles. Richie was still sniffling when the end of recess bell rang. He wiped the tears and snot from his face before he and Jesse got back to class. Sadly, that memory of violence would stick with Jesse for all his life.

Dawson High Day One
It wasn't really the whole first day at Dawson High that was unusual, just the one early morning encounter. Jesse arrived at the high school campus 30 minutes before his first class. When his mom had called the school to enroll him she had insisted on one of the guidance counselors giving Jesse a tour of the school. Of course Jesse hated the idea of being paraded around campus, but there was no arguing with Mrs. Colton when it came to school and educational activities.

Jesse and his mom met Mr. Hannah at his office. For the first few minutes Mr. Hannah and Margo talked in that formal, polite way adults do when they meet for the first time and kids are present.

As Margo starts to go over Jesse's past, Jesse begins to hope she and Mr. Hannah will take the whole 30 minutes and he won't have to go on the here-is-the-new-kid tour.

Unfortunately for Jess, it takes his mom just 10 minutes to cover his schooling, as well as his scores on standard tests for reading, writing, history and math.

Before Margo leaves, she gives Jesse a kiss on the cheek, tells him to have a good first day and reminds him to walk home with his sister, who will be waiting for him at the elementary school.

Mr. Hannah motions for Jesse to join him as he heads out of his office. "Okay, Jesse, let's first find your locker. It's on the second floor of Warren Hall. Then if there's time I'll show you your classes, the auditorium, the gym and the cafeteria." As they leave the administrative building and head towards Jesse's locker, Mr. Hannah asks "Will you bring your lunch ?"

"I dunno. What do most kids do ?"

"Some eat at the cafeteria. Some go off campus. Some bring their lunch. Did you bring a lunch today ?"

"No, but I have some money."

"Then you should try the cafeteria. It's pretty good. I think Salisbury Steak is the main course today."

While they walk across campus Mr. Hannah begins to offer facts. "Warren Hall, the cafeteria and the gymnasium are the original buildings of Dawson High. We've since added McKinley Hall, which is three stories, just like Warren, and the administration building. The admin building also has our auditorium and band room."

They enter Warren Hall through the south entrance. The double doors are pinned open. So are the doors at the north end of the building. Jesse can feel a light breeze once he steps into the hallway. Mr. Hannah continues "Your locker and most of your classes will be on the second floor of this building. You have P.E. with Mr. Phillips for second period, right? That'll be at the gym. Your science class will be over in McKinley hall."

Jesse nods.

They walk past the first classroom and then Mr. Hannah points to the stairway on their left. "Let's head up here."

The stairway is about seven feet wide and has two ninety degree turns before reaching the second floor. There's a landing area at each of the two turns. The handrail is on Jesse's right and the stairwell wall is on the left. While they make the climb, Mr. Hannah asks.

"Do you play any sports or have any interests...any hobbies?"

"Not much. My dad and I throw the football around once in a while and I was on a soccer team for a while when we were in Saudi Arabia..."

"Okay, what about interests or hobbies? We have lots of clubs here."

"I like...drafting and architecture. My uncle is an architect and he always shows me his drawings and sends me pictures of his work. He does cool stuff."

They reach the second floor. Mr. Hannah takes Jesse to his locker, gives him the combination code and shows him how to open it. He also points out the rooms for Jesse's classes.

"We've got a couple more minutes so let's go back downstairs and I'll show you where McKinley and the gym are. We don't have time to go see them, but at least you'll know which way to head for your other classes."

When they head down the stairs Jesse asks "So..what clubs do you have?"

"We have chess, French, math, Spanish, yearbook and a few others. Sorry, no architecture club."

As they descend Jesse hears a female voice say "That's good."

He had been concentrating on his feet and watching the stairs so he didn't notice the three girls at the first stairwell landing. When he heard the voice he stopped and looked up. Two of the girls were holding a poster on the stairwell wall while the third one was watching.

Even though she had her back to Jesse, his initial thought was that she was mocking him about architecture. "Oh, so it's good there's no architecture club ?" he asks her backside.

She turns towards him "What...no." She quickly glances from Jesse to Mr. Hannah and back to Jesse. Sincerely, she says "I was talking about the poster. We want to tape it level. I was telling them "it's good" (she does the finger air quotes with "it's good") as in "it's level" (finger quotes again). She smiles at Jesse for just a second then she half turns toward the poster and points. "It's for the Sadie Hawkins dance in three weeks."

The two other girls pause taping up the poster long enough to glance over at Jesse and Mr. Hannah. One of those girls says "Hi Mr. Hannah. Who's the new kid?"

Jesse thinks "Great, I'm that obvious"

Mr. Hannah nods towards Jesse and begins "This is Jesse. Today's his first day here, but he's been all over the world, Alaska, China, and most recently Saudi Arabia. Now his family has settled in our fair city. Please welcome him." All three of the girls say hi to Jesse. Mr. Hannah goes on "Jesse, this is Susan." he nods towards the girl who asked the question, "This is Tonya." He nods toward the other girl at the poster. "And your architect friend here is Dawn."

Good naturedly, Dawn says "Very funny Mr. H" then she gives Jesse that same smile again. He's a little perplexed by it because her smile is tight lipped, like the fake or forced smile people sometimes offer, but when she talked to him there was no sarcasm in her tone.

She asks Jesse "Do you know what is a Sadie Hawkins dance?" She smiles and takes a half step towards Jesse as she waits for his reply.

Jesse starts to get a little nervous. Not only is she asking him a strange question, but she's getting closer to him. Jesse thinks "Sadie Hawkins dance? No idea". He shakes his head no.

"It's a dance where the girls ask the guys to the dance." She smiles again and takes another half step towards Jesse.

She's getting too close. Jesse fights the urge to step back from her. He feels himself smile in the same tight lipped style as Dawn. He hopes his smile looks genuine, even though he is confused by her.

This time Dawn first steps forward and then talks "As an organizer of the dance, it would be terribly wrong for me to go without a date. And since Mr. H asked us to welcome you I guess I should ask you to the dance."

Dawn pauses and looks at Jesse. Jesse is confused on multiple levels. This girl is standing right in front of him and she's just about close enough to notice his heart trying to explode through his chest. She's got an unusual smile, but it's a smile she shared with him. And did she just ask me to this Sadie Hawkins dance. His brain loops on that last part.

While Jesse works over these points, Tonya and Susan have moved to flanking positions of Dawn. Tonya comments "Dawn, I think you petrified him." Susan follows with "Yeah Dawn. He looks petrified. What did you do?"

"I just asked him to the Sadie Hawkins dance." She turns to Mr. Hannah. "I think I broke the new kid."

"I noticed. Can you unbreak him before class starts?"

Before Dawn can answer, the five-minutes-to-class bell rings. This brings Jesse out of his petrifaction. He first sees Dawn, Tonya and Susan staring at him. All three are smiling in anticipation. He turns to Mr. Hannah who is giving Jesse a 'your move' look.

After another couple of seconds Jesse says to Mr. Hannah "Did she just...."

Mr. Hannah tells him "Yes. Dawn just asked you to the dance. Hurry up and tell her yes so you can get to your very first class on time."

"She really asked..." Jesse looks back at Dawn and sees her smiling and nodding.

"Yes, Jesse. She really asked. I recommend you say yes."

"Yes?"

"Good. Now that that is settled, off to class everyone. Jesse, your class is up." Mr. Hannah points upstairs. The girls seem to be talking and giggling as they head down stairs. Jesse heads to his class.

For the rest of the day Jesse looks for Dawn every chance he gets but doesn't see her. He begins to wonder if it all was a joke being played on the new kid. Maybe she doesn't even go to Dawson High. Maybe she was just helping friends decorate for the dance, but she really goes to some cross town high school and decided to trip a newbie.

At the end of the day Jesse goes to drop off books at his locker. When he opens it, a note falls to the floor. He picks it and reads it "Meet me at the dance banner tomorrow morning 10 minutes before classes start. Dawn ☺"

One of the things Jesse's efficiency expert dad liked to tell Jesse was "It's important to consider the possibilities, but it is just as important to consider the impossibilities" His dad's words entered Jesse's mind as he re-read Dawn's note. On his walk home Jesse considered possibilities and impossibilities. He thinks "What does she want? Does she want to back out of the dance? Possibly. Did she find someone else to go with her? Possibly. Maybe she doesn't really go to Dawson...possibly, but she left a note in my locker...and how did she find my locker ? If she found my locker she must like me. Maybe she already wants to go steady..Possibly! Yes!! " "Impossibility sounds more likely" Alice chimes in from beside him.

In his bubble of concentration regarding tomorrow's meeting with Dawn, Jesse failed to notice that he was talking out loud and that his little sister had joined him as he passed by her elementary school.

As they continuing walking the 2 blocks to their rental house, Jesse looks down at his sister and says playfully "Oh..it's not so impossible. She did ask me to a dance the very first time she saw me. I'd say she found me irresistible."

Alice makes a slight gagging sound then says "When Mr. Whiskers and I invite you to our tea party it's not because of your irresistibility. It's because Ms. Bear Bear needs a partner. We need a fourth for our tea."

With raised eye browses Jesse says "Hey! What makes you so sure Ms. Bear Bear doesn't find me irresistible?"

"Because she's a stuffed bear... and because she only talks to me."

"Oh..Does she ever ask about me ?"

"No"

"Does she ever inquire about my health?"

"No"

"Does she ever ask how soon I'll get my license so I can take her to a movie?"

"No, and besides, you're not old enough to drive."

"Wrongo. Mom has already signed me up for driver's training. I'll be driving by January..then look out ladies."

"Driving around in what? Mom's minivan?" As Alice asks these poignant questions, she turns from the sidewalk to the walkway up to their front door. Jesse stops on the sideway in front of their house and looks at his mom's leased minivan in the driveway. It's big and boxy. It's a dull, dreary silver. He asks himself "Could driving a minivan possibly be cool?" He knows the answer is as obvious as the sound of Alice closing the front door.

The next morning Jesse left home 15 minutes early. When he got to the banner he saw Dawn coming around the corner at the far end of the hall. She gives a quick wave and easy smile as she walks up. She says

"Hi. I'm glad you got my note."

"Me, too....what's up?"

"You're a junior, right ?"

Jesse replies "Yep" as he wonders how she knows this.

"I didn't think of it yesterday, but then I realized Mr. Hannah is the guidance counselor for juniors. My counselor is Misses Kurtz because I'm a sophomore." She continues "We don't have any classes together and I have band practice at lunch. I know this will sound weird."

Jesse feels fear start to creep up his spine. His irresistibility index is ready to plunge. He thinks "I hope she doesn't want out".

After a brief pause, she says "This Saturday I'm going to Sharks' Tooth Mountain with my mom and little brother. Do you want to come with us? It's not that far out of town and my mom wants to see who I'm going to the dance with."

Jesse quickly thinks "She's asking me out again. This is great!" He doesn't realize he hasn't answered Dawn until she asks "Is your smile a yes, then?"

"Oh, yeah..I mean yes, but two questions. What is Sharks' Tooth Mountain and how do we get there?"

"It's a mountain, well, more like a hilly area, where you can find fossilized teeth of sharks. You'll see when we get there."

"Okay."

"We can pick you up at 9 on Saturday...if that's not too early."

"That's fine. Do I need to bring anything?"

"Nah, mom has plenty of tools. What's your address?"

"Douglas, 365 Douglas. Know it?"

"Sure, I know where it is."

The bell signaling 5 minutes to first period rings.

"So...we will pick up on Saturday."

Jesse nods and watches as she turns and heads back down the hall.

She is three steps away when he suddenly realizes he has to babysit Alice on Saturday. In a panic, he shouts "Can I bring my little sister? Oh, and what is your locker number ?"

She turns to look at him. She has that intriguing tight lipped smile. Then she says "Sure. How old is she?"

"She's ten...but she acts like she's the boss"

"Great. Bring her. She can play with my brother. He's ten and acts like he knows everything. They'll get along swimmingly. Oh, and if I can find your locker, you should be able to find mind." As she turns to leave she smiles that same smile and says "Good luck." Jesse notices there' a flash of something, not predatory, but more challenging in her expression. She's having fun playing with him.

As Jesse stands there the first period bell rings. His class is the first room on the second floor. While he climbs the stairs he thinks about Dawn, their two dates, and finding her locker.

Finding Dawn's Locker

On Friday morning of his first week at Dawson High, home of the Crimson Daredevils, Jesse stops by Mr. Hannah's office. The door is open and Mr. Hannah is at his desk. Jesse knocks on the door frame and when Mr. Hannah looks up, Jesse says

"Good mornin' Mr. Hannah. I just wanted to say thanks for the tour on Monday."

Mr. Hannah smiles and asks "How's your first week going ?"

"Okay...so far. Math and history has been stuff I already know."

"Good. So classes are okay ?"

Jesse nods. Mr. Hannah continues "Are you making new friends, besides Dawn?"

"Not yet. But speaking of Dawn, do you know where her locker is?"

"I don't. But can't you just ask her?"

"She's...uhm...challenged me to find her locker"

"Oh. That's novel of her. Well, I guess I can help you a little bit. Since she's a sophomore her locker will be on the first floor of McKinley hall."

"Can't you look up the number or something?"

"I probably could..." he glances at the wall clock, then continues slowly, pausing between each word "but   there's just   no   time". Right when he says 'time' the first period bell rings. Quickly, Mr Hannah says "Have a good day, Jesse. " He nods a good-bye to Jesse and then moves his focus to the papers on his desk. Jesse drops his head in disappointment as only a teen age boy can do, then he turns and shuffles off to his class.

He really wants to find Dawn's locker before tomorrow so he can impress her while they are at the mountain. On the walk to his class he comes up with a simple plan. Camp out in the sophomore locker area all lunch and even after school, if necessary. Surely Dawn will stop by her locker during one of those times, even if she has band practice at lunch.

When the final morning class session ends, Jesse hustles to the first floor of McKinley. Kids are still spilling out of the classrooms when Jesse takes up a lookout point at the south doorway. He knows the majority of the students will exit that way since the cafeteria and quad area are in that direction.

Jesse starts glancing back and forth between the kids walking past him as they exit McKinley and those kids standing at or approaching lockers along the hallway. Dawn is not in the crowd that goes by Jesse. After they are gone, he walks down the hallway to get a better look at the students lingering around the lockers. Jesse can tell none of them are Dawn, but he sees two of her friends, Tonya and Susan. He approaches them just in time to hear Tonya say rather empathically to the boy in front of her "For the last time, Edgar, I'm not asking you to the dance....you're just too....Edgar" With that she and Susan just as empathically turn and leave before noticing Jesse. As they walk away Jesse manages to offer a rather weak "Hi" to them but they don't hear him.

Jesse and Edgar watch the girls walk out the doorway. Once the girls are gone Jesse turns to Edgar. They stand looking at each other for too long, each expecting the other one to speak. The awkward silence is broken when Edgar says in a dreamy voice "She's my soul mate. She just doesn't know it yet." The awkward silence returns, enhanced by Edgar's comment. This time Jesse breaks it. "That's great. Say, do you know Tonya's friend, Dawn?"

Edgar thinks, then replies "Dawn...Oh, you mean 'Megalodon'."

"Megalodon?"

"Yeah, Megalodon. She's a sophomore, average height, kinda thin, with straight black hair to her shoulder and black eyes. I mean...her irises have no color."

Sounding a bit confused and unsure, Jesse replies "That sounds like her, like Dawn. Why do you call her megalodon?"

"You know what a megalodon is, right ? A shark, a prehistoric shark."

"Okay, but why call Dawn that ?"

"Let's see…her last name is Sharky, but that's not really why. It's because when she kisses, she doesn't close her eyes. Instead, her eyes roll back in her head, just like a shark does when it attacks. Oh, and there's the bite mark her ex-boyfriend showed everyone right after they broke up. It was just one bite on his shoulder, but there were multiple sets of teeth marks like she had two or three rows of teeth. It was pretty creepy to look at, or so I heard."

Jesse doesn't say anything right away because he is categorizing each thing Edgar told him. Last name of Sharky. I can't argue with that. Must be true. Rolls her eyes back when she kisses. That sounds a bit odd, but hopefully I find out for myself at the dance, maybe even tomorrow …but probably not since her mom and my little sister will be there. Rumored to have multiple sets of teeth. Never heard of such a thing, plus it seems impossible. No human can fit two or three rows of teeth in their mouth.

Then Jesse remembers Dawn's smile, tight lipped so no teeth are showing. And that almost predatory look she gave him. What was that look about? His mind flashes to a time 10 years ago when he and his mom were standing in the grocery store checkout line. A tall, thin man with pale skin and almost pointy ears got in line behind them. Jesse couldn't help but stare at him. When the man noticed Jesse watching him he raised his right hand, palm towards Jesse and as he made a V shape with two fingers on one side of the V and two on the other side he said stoically "Live long and prosper my young human friend". Jesse had just seen a Vulcan. He was sure of it until a couple months later he saw the man working as a waiter at the local pancake house. In a much more human voice, the man said to Jesse "Hey kid, how ya doin' today?"

How often are first impressions wrong ? Does that mean Edgar's story about Dawn are more or less likely to be true? He doesn't know, but he still wants to find her locker. Finally he asks Edgar "Do you know where her locker is?"

"Oh sure. It's right here, next to Tonya's. It's number 204."

"204? You sure?"

"I see her here with Tonya, usually in the morning before class."

Jesse thinks 'Alright, mission accomplished. WooHoo!' To Edgar he says "Thanks...see you later."

As Jesse heads towards the cafeteria Edgar says, half to Jesse, half to himself "Yay, see you later...I'm gonna hang out here. I know Tonya will be back soon."

Sharks' Tooth Mountain

At 9:09am Saturday Jesse opens the front door right before Dawn pushes the door bell.

"Hey, no fair. I wanted to hear your door bell."

"Well go ahead."

She pushes the buzzer mounted on the door frame and they both hear a typical ding-dong.

From somewhere inside the house Alice asks "Jesse, is that your girlfriend at the door ?"

Jesse rolls his eyes then quickly looks at Dawn to see if she heard Alice. He can't tell for sure because Dawn is now rummaging in her purse for something. He ignores Alice's comment. He looks past Dawn and asks

"Is that your mom?"

"Yep, that's my mom and that's our gigantic, vintage '77 Ford station wagon."

"I don't see your brother? Is he coming with us?"

"He's there. He's just slouched down in the front seat."

Alice announces her arrival with "Hi. I'm Alice". She offers her hand to Dawn.

Dawn shakes her hand and replies "Hi Alice. I'm Dawn. Pleased to meet you."

"Are we really going to find sharks' teeth?"

"Oh, I guarantee it. You'll come home with at least one shark's tooth."

"How about we get going?" Jess asks.

Dawn nods and they all head for the wagon. When they get near the car, she says "We can all fit in the back seat." She walks around to the driver side and opens the back seat door. Alice has followed her and dives in first, then Dawn. Meanwhile, Jesse has gotten in on the passenger side. Dawn's mom turns in her seat so she can see Jesse and Alice. "Good morning" she says to both of them. They reply with "Good morning". Dawn adds "Mom, this is Jesse, and his sister Alice. Jess, Alice, this is my mom."

Once Jesse's mom found out he and Alice were invited on this Saturday excursion with Dawn and her mom, Mrs. Colton had done a little background checking while attending her first PTA meeting. She didn't tell Jess all she had heard, but she felt it was safe for her kids to go with Dawn and her mom. She told Jesse and Alice to be sure to thank Mrs. Sharky for allowing them to go. When Dawn finished her introduction, both Jesse and Alice said "Thank you for inviting us, Mrs. Sharky."

As Mrs. Sharky turns forward and puts the car in gear, she replies "You're very welcome. And please, call me Debbie. Buckle up, everyone, we are on the road."

Once they pull away from the curb Mrs. Sharky glances over to the front passenger seat and says "Rex, that means you, too. Sit up and put on your seat belt...and say hi to our guests."

Jesse hears the click of a seat belt, but he doesn't see anyone in the passenger seat. He looks over at Dawn and she motions for him to take another look. When he looks back at the seat in front of him he is met by the snarling face of an angry Tyrannous Rex peeking over the seat back. The head is only about the size of an egg, but it's not at all what Jesse was expecting. The mouth is partially open, exposing an armada of pointy teeth. The eyes are red with fury and below the flaring nostrils is a carefully drawn handlebar mustache. "A swashbuckling dinosaur?" Jesse asks himself.

Without moving its mouth, the dinosaur says "My name is Reginald, but everyone calls me Rex. I am an anthropologist. I study the past, present and future. Shark's Tooth mountain is my favorite place to study the past. If you find any teeth or bones, give them to me and I won't eat you."

Mrs. Sharky interrupts "Okay Rex, behave. Please sit up and say hi to our guests."

The dinosaur disappears below the seat back with an accompanying "Bye bye". Up pops the head of a young boy. He twists toward the back seat and says a quick 'Hi'. Jesse says "Hi". Alice whispers to Jesse "He's too short, I can't see him."

It's quiet for the next 5 minutes except for Mrs. Sharky humming along to a Jim Croce's "Time in a bottle" playing on the car radio.

When the song is over the radio station goes to commercial break so she turns down the volume and asks Jesse where he is from. He explains he was born in Texas, but his family has moved a lot because of his dad's work. When Jesse mentions they lived in China, Mrs. Sharky interjects "I'd love to go to China. There are so many fossils sites there and more are being discovered all the time. Did you go to museums or visit any archeology sites?"

"No, we didn't go to any archeological sites... but we did go to some museums and stuff. Our mom always wants us to meet local people, try local food and explore local culture, as she calls it. She had me and Alice join local clubs. Mom found an architecture club for me and Alice join a ballet club."

In a wishful voice Alice says "I love ballet dancing" She hums Pachelbel's Canon in D as she moves her arms through the first 5 ballet positions.

"Nicely done" Dawn says to her.

Alice adds "I still write to Wen. She was in my ballet club. She's my best friends."

Mrs. Sharky asks "How did your mom find an architecture and ballet club in China?"

Jesse answers "I don't know. She's very ..uuh..resourceful. She finds all kinds of things wherever we go. She found all kinds of clubs there. Ping Pong, chess, our clubs, running clubs, dog clubs, turtle clubs, bike clubs"

"Turtle clubs?" Rex asks

Jesse and Alice exchange measured looks at each other, then Jesse answers "Yea, it's for kids and adults who like turtles. I think everyone takes their favorite turtles to the meetings and they all talk about turtles and stuff."

"I see." Mrs. Sharky replies.

"Did they have any other food clubs?" Rex asks.

"Rex!"

"Mom, I'm an anthropologist. I've heard of turtle soup"

Now Alice joins in "We never had turtle soup, but Jesse sure liked what they call 'fin soup'. He'd go over to his girlfriend's house and her mom would make it for him every time he visited. He liked the soup more than the girl."

"Yeah! That's not true. She wasn't my girlfriend." Jesse protests.

Both Dawn and Mrs. Sharky are smiling at Jesse's slight discomfort. To ease things Mrs. Sharky announces "We'll be there in a couple minutes. Dawn, why don't explain what we will do."

"Sure, mom. First off, Shark Tooth Mountain isn't really a mountain. It's more like a bunch of barren hills. Some are rolling, like big mounds of smoothed over dirt and some are steeper, with ravines and crevices. There's no plants there, except a few wild flowers in the spring. The ground is way too hard to dig into with a regular shovel so we use mattocks. They're sort of like handheld ice picks, but one end of head has a blade about two inches wide. Archeologists ...and some gardeners, use them for turning over small areas of the ground. We brought extras so you and Alice can have your own.

"The best places to find shark's teeth are where other people have already been digging. Since the ground is broken there, it's easier digging. We usually spread out to start with. Each of us goes excavating and if anyone starts to find teeth or other artifacts, we call the others over. It's fun to dig together once you start finding things. You'll see. Did you really like the soup more than the girl?

Jesse contemplates the question. After two seconds he smacks his lips a couple times and gives a definite "Yes, now that I think about it, I did. You see, it wasn't just a bowl of soup." He pauses, then continues "It had... a fragrance, a haunting bouquet... that would linger in my nose long after I swallowed the broth.

Jesse's eyes are closed and he's lifted his nose as if he's searching for the scent. "It only had mushrooms and fins, but they combined with Mrs. Lin's broth to make a soup I'd marry if I could.

Alice and Dawn giggle at this while the car comes to a stop. Mrs. Sharky announces "We're here." Jesse opens his eyes and turns towards the giggling girls. Dawn says "You were out there." Alice adds "Yea, way out there, soup boy."

Mrs. Sharky is opening the wagon's back gate when the rest of them join her. From a canvas bag she pulls out mattock after mattock, handing them to Jesse, Alice, Dawn and Rex. She pulls out one more for herself. From her purse she pulls out 5 new plastic sandwich baggies and distributes them.

Mrs. Sharky addresses Jesse and Alice. "The baggies are for anything you want to keep. Now since this is your first time here...and we don't want to lose you, we are going to team up. Rex, you'll start off with Jesse. Dawn, you'll take Alice." Both Dawn and Jesse look disappointed. "I know you two wanted to team up and you'll get that chance later, but for now this is the arrangements." She turns to her son. "Rex, take Jesse to the east hill. Maybe there's some new digs there. And remember, a good anthropologist doesn't talk down about his sister. He talks about her good qualities...her human qualities."

"Got it, mom" Rex says quickly and then nods for Jesse to follow him. As they are walking away Rex asks Jesse "Have I told you about the time Dawn laughed so hard she peed her pants?"

Dawn begins to raise her mattock over her head, but not in a serious way. Mrs. Sharky says "Okay, why don't you girls come with me? We can dig and talk." They head west.

After almost an hour and half of digging and scraping, the girls haven't found anything exciting. They decide to go back to the wagon for a break. After they rest for a minute Dawn says "I'll go get Rex and Jesse." Alice says "I'll go with you."

Mrs. Sharky rests on the station wagon's tailgate and watches the girls head east. The girls are just about to disappear around the first bend in the path when Rex and Jesse come walking towards them. The four of them congregate for a minute, then Rex steps away from the other three. He raises his arms up over his head, with his elbows extended out and his finger tips just touching. He makes a big zero. It's his way of signaling to his mom that they didn't find any teeth. Mrs. Sharky waves back to him so he knows she saw him.

Now the four of them head to the car. When they are about 100 yards from the station wagon Dawn says "I want to talk with Rex for a minute. You guys go ahead."

Jesse and Alice walk on while Dawn and Rex hang back. Dawn asks Rex "Did you guys find any teeth at all?"

"No. Nothing. Just plain old dirt and gravel. Why?"

"I told Alice we would find shark's teeth for sure."

"Yeah, well, life's full of disappointments."

"I know, but she's so sweet and I promised her. Maybe I can give her one of mine."

"Bad idea! You know mom doesn't want you doing that."

"I've got plenty, and I'll have more as I get older, I'm sure."

"Don't do it."

Dawn drops her mattock and her plastic bag right at Rex's feet. She bends over to get them. With her head level to Rex's torso, she turns to him and pleds "Rex, help me, please. I want to give Alice a tooth. I know she will love it and I promise I won't ask you to do it ever again."

By now Jesse and Alice are at the car. Mrs. Sharky hands Jesse a cup of water. He drinks it as he turns to check on Dawn and Rex. Rex has his back towards Jesse. Dawn is on the far side of Rex and she's bent over, probably reaching for her mattock that's on the ground. Jesse sees Rex's shoulder lurch toward Dawn, almost like the Alaskan bully's motion, but he thinks that can't be right. Jesse is startled to see Dawn go down on one knee. He's confused, just like in Alaska, but this time he doesn't just stand there. He starts walking towards Dawn. He's gone about 10 feet when he sees Dawn pick up her mattock, her baggy and after a pause, she picks up something too small for Jesse to see. Jesse has stopped so he can better watch what they are doing.

Dawn stands up and hands the item to Rex. She rubs the lower part of her face as she and Rex look at the item for a second. He hands it back to her. Then they head towards the car. Jesse watches as they approach. When they are close enough, Dawn says "Hey Alice, I got a nice shark's tooth for you. Rex and I just found it on the ground back there." She holds it up, between her thumb and index finger. When she walks past Jesse she tilts her head and gives him her tight-lipped smile again as if to say all is good.

Alice had been sitting on the wagon's tailgate, sipping her cup of water and talking with Mrs. Sharky. At the news from Dawn, she let out a 'Yes' as she hops off the gate. She starts to run towards Dawn, but Dawn was just two steps away. Alice practically bumps into Dawn as Dawn says "Check it out." and she hands the tooth to Alice.

"Wow! That's so cool." Alice admires it. She holds it the same way Dawn did, but she turns and twists her wrist so she can see it from all angles. Then she says "Jess, look at the size of it...and look how white it is" Before Jess can reply Rex jumps in with "It's about normal size for a young shark of that type. A full grown one will have teeth about 50% bigger."

Jesse replies "How can a fossilized tooth be that white? It looks...' he glances at Dawn "..new"

Dawn says "Take a look at my mom's teeth."

Mrs. Sharky is smiling a big broad smile. Her teeth are even whiter. Then she pulls out a leather necklace from under her shirt. It has three shark's teeth on it and they are just as white as Alice's new tooth. "I got these three beauties the same way Dawn got that one."

Jesse looks away from Mrs. Sharky's teeth. He takes a sip of water while he tries not to think the thoughts that are popping into his brain. Thoughts that are too ridiculous to even consider keep biting on his mind. He knows those clearly are shark's teeth. He tells himself he just hasn't seen fossilized teeth before. He will look up pictures of fossilized shark's teeth when he gets home. As he takes another sip of water he peers over the cups lid to check out Alice's new tooth and the teeth on Mrs. Sharky's necklace.

A car door closes and from inside the station wagon Rex announces "Mom, I have to go to the bathroom. Can we get going?"

All the way home Jesse keeps replaying in this mind the scene of Dawn bent over, then Rex appearing to throw a punch at her, then Dawn going down on one knee and picking up.what? The tooth? He watches it over and over in his mind, but still can't make sense of it. He's completely forgotten he and Dawn were going to dig for teeth together.

He is so zoned out not only does he not see they are parked in front of his house, but he doesn't hear Mrs. Sharky the first time she says "It was nice meeting both of you." Alice has to tug on his sleeve to pull him back to reality. "What?" he says. Mrs. Sharky repeats herself "It was nice meeting both of you."

"Oh, right. It was nice meeting you, too, Mrs. Sharky. And you Rex." He looks at Dawn but doesn't say anything right away. He's half way out the car door when he pauses, turns to her and says "Thanks. That was fun."

Alice says "That was great. Thanks for the shark's tooth, Dawn." She holds up the plastic bag with the tooth in it. "Can you show me how to make a necklace like your mom has?" "Sure, but first you have to ask your mom." Alice slides across the bench seat and out the same door Jesse used. She runs towards the house, already asking her mom before she even gets inside. Jesse closes the car door. As they start to drive off, Dawn says "See you at school." Jesse smiles and waves good bye to them.

Sadie Hawkins Dance

The Dawson High Daredevil's Sadie Hawkins dance is on the first Friday in November. It is not considered a formal occasion. In reality, it is almost the opposite of a formal dance. Some of the kids dress in the excessively rural style of Dogpatch residences. There are always some guys going as L'il Abner and girls as Daisy Mae. Not surprisingly, no one ever dresses up as the dance's namesake, Sadie Hawkins.

For the dance Jesse wanted to pick up Dawn, but Dawn insisted Sadie Hawkins tradition requires her to pick him up. Since Dawn wasn't old enough to drive, it meant another ride with Dawn and her mom.

Jesse knew exactly what he wanted to wear. The white slacks he got while in Saudi Arabia and a red silk shirt from China. Along with those he wore his pitch black canvas high top tennis shoes he got right after they settled in Bakersfield, and his dad's white dress jacket. He didn't look like anyone you'd see in the comic strip but he liked the red and white combination, with the touch of black provided by his new shoes.

When he finished dressing he went into the living room with the intention of looking out the front window, but his mom blocked his way. When she saw him walk into the room, she sprang up off the sofa, stepped in front of him and exclaimed "Mr. Colton, who is this handsome young man in our house?" From the study Mr. Colton replies "What's that, Margo?" In a quiet voice Jesse's mom tells Jesse "You do look handsome, son. Your father's jacket fits you nicely." Then in a louder voice she says "Mr. Colton, come see your son before he goes off to his first dance." "Thanks, mom." Jesse responds genuinely to her compliment

The creak of the office chair tells Jesse and his mom Mr. Colton is on his way. After a brief pause Mr. Colton steps into the living room then stops a few feet away from Jesse. As he looks his son over he says "Well, well son, I see you have the suave Colton style I made famous throughout much of Texas and Louisiana while I was dating your mom."

"Paah-shaw, the one time you dressed like this was when you took me to the roller derby."

The doorbell rings and Jesse quickly moves to answer it. He opens the door and sees Dawn. She's wearing a Daisy-Mae inspired red-with-black polka dots blouse and a knee length black skirt. Earlier in the day she had described her outfit to Jesse, but he had been watching her talk more than listening to what she said. Seeing her dressed up, he was stunned by how wonderful she looked.

Jesse didn't realize his mom had joined him until she says "You must be freezing out there, child. Come inside."

Dawn hurriedly steps inside. As she goes past the unmoving Jesse she says softly, playfully "Stuck again?"

Mrs. Colton introduces herself to Dawn and walks her into the living room. She asks Dawn if she'd like to borrow a sweater or wrap. Dawn says no thank you and explains it will be warm at the dance and she will be fine. Jesse joins them. Dawn says to Jesse "We better get going. Mom is waiting and I should be at the dance since I'm one of the organizers." To Mrs. Colton she says "Nice to meet you, Mrs. Colton." Jesse and Dawn head towards the front door, but before they leave Jesse turns to his mom and says "Good night, mom." She smiles and nods to him.

The ride to the dance is quick and quiet. Jesse and Mrs. Sharky say hi to each other. Jesse asks about Rex and Mrs. Sharky says he's at home, reviewing his fossil collection. After that it's just the radio until they get to the high school. As Jesse and Dawn start to get out opposite sides of the car Mrs. Sharky asks "What time do I pick you up?" "Eleven, mom" Dawn replies. "Okay, I'll be right here at eleven, then. Have fun" Dawn and Jesse close their doors and Mrs. Sharky drives off.

In the cool night air they walk with the purpose of getting inside gym, where the dance and warmth await them. They are not the first to arrive, but once Dawn has given their tickets to the lady at the door, they can see there are just a few people inside the decorated gym.

Jesse stops and looks around. There are a few more posters like the one he saw Dawn and her friends hanging in the stairwell. In wonder, he asks "Wow, did you do all this?" Dawn smiles and says "We worked on it after school and over a couple weekends."

On cue, Tonya and Susan appear and start talking quickly to Dawn. Tonya explains "The DJ hasn't shown up. He should have been here 30 minutes ago. He should of been set up already!" Susan adds "If we don't have music tonight...we don't have a party. And everyone knows we're this year's organizers"

All three girls' expressions turn to fear as the possibility their dance may become a disaster starts to well up in them.

Jesse hears all they say and sees their expressions. He asks "Does this DJ bring his own sound system? Or does he use the gym's PA system?"

"They always bring their own speakers and stuff." Dawn answers.

"Well, if we could use the PA system for the music, then all we would need is a DJ...oh, and music, of course"

Dawn says "The PA system is" Tonya jumps in with "pretty sucky"

"It's definitely better than nothing" Susan says. Then she says "Let's go find Mr. Hannah and see if he will let us use it. Maybe he can hook it up to a radio station."

As the girls walk away, Jesse notices the two guys that had been hanging back. They step up to Jesse. "Hey, Jesse." Edgar says. "Edgar" Jesse says and gives him a nod. "So Tonya finally asked you?" "Yay, I just happened to be hanging out near her locker at the end of the day today." To the other teenager, Jesse says "I'm Jesse." "I'm Mark." He says as they shake hands. After a pause, Mark continues " Ya'know, when Edgar says he just happened to hanging out near Tonya's locker he means he happened to be there the same way day happens to end in a 'y'"

As Mark says this, he and Jesse look at Edgar. Edgar gives them a "Yay, I know" shrug and then looks down at his shoes.

Mark askes Jesse "So..you're here with Dawn?"

"Yep" Jesse replies.

At that, Mark starts to walk away, at least that's the way it looks to Jesse. It turns out Mark was just stepping back, then walking around Jesse. Jesse feels an odd obligation to stand still as he is inspected. Once Mark returns to his starting spot he puts on a thoughtful look and says "I don't see any bite marks. How about you, Edgar?" "Nope" Edgar responds. Mark presses the side of his right index finger to his lips, adding to his thoughtful look, then he says "No bites...so I'm guessing you haven't been on any dates with Megladon."

Defensively, Jesse blurts out "Yes I have. We went to Shark's Tooth Mountain together!"

"Oh, Shark's Tooth Mountain. With Megladon! And you came back alive!!" Mark just barely gets 'alive' out before bursting into laughter. He's shaking his head in disbelief so he doesn't notice the girls are just getting back.

"What's so funny?" Dawn asks.

Jesse replies "Mark was just enjoying the fact that we went to Shark's Tooth Mountain together." After giving Mark a hard look, Jesse takes on a calm demeanor and asks Dawn "What did Mr. Hannah say?"

"He said he already called the DJ about 15 minutes ago and the guy is on his way."

After a few seconds of silence Edgar says "Tonya, did your mom really make Shmoo shaped cookies?"

"Ten dozen. On the table" she says as she motions toward the table over on the right side of the gym. Everyone looks over at the table. Jesse, in a low voice, asks Dawn "Shmoo? ", but before she can explain the Shmoo there is a loud banging on the side door next to the table.

"That must be the DJ" says Susan. "That better be the DJ" Dawn says more emphatically. She starts walking towards the door. Everyone else follows.

Mr. Hannah is at the door first. He unlocks and opens it as the kids get there. Before the guy is even half way through the door he announces in a clear, confident voice "DJ Ricky has arrived!". "And late!" says Tonya and Susan simultaneously. In a more normal voice Ricky replies "Sorry, kids. Car trouble. Any of you want to help me get set up?" With their help, DJ Ricky is up and running in about 5 minutes.

Even though DJ Ricky was late, he has done enough high school dances that he knows the biggest challenge. No matter what the theme or occasion may be, getting kids started, getting them out on the floor for that initial dance is always the hardest part of the gig. Once that first couple is out there and dancing, others will follow.

He has worked out a routine that continues to get him bookings. Play the first song, either "Dance To The Music" by Sly and the Family Stone, or "Celebration" by Kool and the Gang. If that doesn't bring anyone out, Ricky goes to the next step. It might seem a little devious when he does it, but by the end of the night what people remember is he got the dancing started.

Every high school dance has organizers. Someone stepped up and did the decorating, the coordinating, and promoting of the dance. The organizers have put in a lot of effort and they want their dance to be a success. Like the Sadie Hawkins dance tonight, it's usually a couple girls.

With no one on the dance floor at the end of "Celebration", DJ Ricky employs step two. On the mic he says "Welcome, everyone, to the Dawson High Sadie Hawkins dance. This place looks great! How about a hand to your dance organizers?" Ricky looks down to consult the back of a business card as a few of the kids clap. "Dawn, Tonya, and Susan, can you step onto the dance floor ? And bring your dates, too."

Since the girls and their dates had just helped Ricky get set up, they were right next to him. Ricky is looking at them and that draws everyone else's attention to the group. Off the mic, Ricky says to them "Go on" and nods his head towards the dance floor.

Jesse feels Dawn take his hand and start towards to dance floor. Jesse has given a lot of thought to this night. Being asked out by Dawn. Going on his first real date. Sitting next to her in her mom's car. Holding hands and looking into her eyes. He found so much excitement. All these thoughts had been swirling around his teenage mind, but with the tug of his hand by Dawn he suddenly realizes he is going to have to dance...in front of other people.

There is a lightness that travels from his hand held by Dawn to his heart, but there is a heaviness that travels from his head to his suddenly reluctant feet. Sometimes this is called flight vs fight but for Jesse it's dance with Dawn versus stand there. He knows this is a pivot point. He knows he has done enough standing already. As he steps toward her, DJ Ricky announces "Here's Dance To The Music".

Jesse is dancing, at least he thinks he is. He feels his body moving, but what he mostly notices is Dawn. She moves with a simple confidence and grace. Her movements have a rhythm that fits the music. She is in constant motion, with her head and shoulders leading the rest of her body through a series of smooth, side to side, actions.

Jesse hadn't noticed that his own dance movements had become more conservative, more restrained, as he watched Dawn, but she must have noticed. She starts clapping along to the music and at the same time encourages Jesse to join in. He does, and so do the kids around them. The clapping gives Jesse a better sense of timing. He now feels like he is closer to actually dancing, and not going through some awkward version of dodgeball-like stunts. He even says "Hey, I'm dancing!" To which Dawn replies with a small nod and a big smile.

DJ Ricky keeps the music going. He plays another three songs without interruption. Dawn keeps Jesse on the dance floor for all the songs. DJ Ricky introduces the next song "Alright, everybody's looking good. Y'all having fun?" The kids around them cheer, but Jesse and Dawn quietly smile at each other. Ricky continues "Good...good. Let's keep it going. Here's Saturday Night Fever. Point if you must."

Later on it is a surprise to Jesse when DJ Ricky announces "This is your last dance, kids. Sadie Hawkins tradition says girls, you should dance this one with your date. Everybody on the dance floor for the Beatles' Twist and Shout."

Jesse and Dawn, along with everyone else, including Mr Hannah, are on the dance floor, shoulders and elbows going in one direction while knees and feet twist in the other. DJ Ricky is the only one not out there, but even he is getting in a little twisting as he starts to pack up some of his gear.

"Alright, kids. It's been blast but we are done for tonight. My name is DJ Ricky. Give me a call for your next party. I've got flyers here so come take one. Until next time, keep dancing."

Some kids had started to leave as Ricky was talking, but once Mr. Hannah turned on the gym lights, most everyone headed for the exit.

Dawn, Tonya and Susan went into clean up mode. Tonya and Susan started taking down the posters and streamers. Dawn went to the drink and cookie table where she started throwing away used cups. When Jesse got there to help her she asked him to dump the leftover punch. When he got back from taking the bowl to empty in the restroom Dawn had retrieved a cardboard box from under the table. Jesse put the punch bowl in the box, then together, they put the unused plates, napkins and cups in the box.

Earlier in the evening Jesse had gotten Dawn and himself cups of punch, but he didn't notice the cookies on the table. Now he sees them. They have an odd shape for a cookie, kind of like a stomach with feet and two frosting eyes at the esophagus. Looking down at them, he asks "Hey, are those the shmookies?" With her hand over her mouth, Dawn laughs, then says "Not shmookies. Shmoo cookies. Two words." "They're a weird shape." "No, they're shmoo shaped." Still perplexed, Jesse asks "What's a shmoo?" Before Dawn can explain, Edgar, who had quietly joined them, replies "Nothing's shmoo. What's shmoo with you?" and then laughs at his own wittiness. Dawn shakes her head at his bad humor then she explains. "The shmoo is a character from the Li'l Abner comic strip. They come from the Valley of the Shmoon. In Li'l Abner's world, they taste like chicken but tonight they taste like sugar cookies."

Dawn picks one up and quickly bites into it, snapping off the head and neck. She smiles at Jesse as she chews on it. She hands him the body of the cookie and says "Try it." After a pause, he takes it and slowly lifts it to his mouth. His motion is slowed because his mind is busy trying to process what he thinks he just saw. When Dawn took her bite...did she have pointed teeth ? Shark's teeth ?

Jesse hears Edgar make a sound that is somewhere between an 'Oh' of surprise and an 'Aha' of fear. Jesse turns to Edgar and sees Edgar's face has gone a bit red. Without prompting, Edgar says "Nothing. It was nothing" and then he quickly grabs a cookie and takes a bite.

When Jesse turns back towards Dawn, she is putting the last of the cookies into a plastic bag. She looks at Jesse and asks "Aren't you going to try it." Jesse takes a bite of the cookie and after a couple chews he says "Hmmm, sugary. Very sugary." Edgar asks "Would you go so far as to say it's shmoogary?" He again laughs at his own humor. This time both Dawn and Jesse, as they look at each other, crack reluctant smiles and shake their heads.

Tonya, Susan, Mark and Mr. Hannah show up. Mr. Hannah asks "You three done?" As she puts the plastic bag of cookies in the box, Dawn replies "Yep. Everything is boxed up." Mr. Hannah reaches for box and says "I'll take that. Mark and Jesse, can you fold up the table and follow me to the office. The rest of you wait for us by the exit."

A minute later they are all standing just inside the exit. Mr. Hannah tells them "It's cold out there so I want to make sure you all have rides waiting for you before I leave. Let's go to the parking lot together and if your ride isn't there I'll come back inside with you and we will go check a few minutes later."

As soon as they step outside it's clear Mr. Hannah knew what he was talking about. The girls immediately pull their arms into their torsos and the guys bury their hands in their pants' pockets. Fortunately, it is a short walk to the parking lot.

There are two cars in the lot, both with their engine running. "Dad's here" says Tonya. In a chattering voice Edgar manages to say "Nnnnice". Tonya and Edgar, along with Susan and Mark, head for the car. Mr. Hannah asks "Can all four of you fit in that little thing?" They don't hear him as they are now focused on getting to the car.

Dawn and Jesse see Mrs. Sharky's big wagon. "There's our ride, Mr. Hannah" Dawn says. She and Jesse quickly head towards the car. Part way there Dawn turns to the kids just about to squeeze into the small car and says "That was a great dance! See you guys on Monday." Then she turns and runs for the car, where Jesse has a door open for her.

Dawn gets in and slides all the way over to the far side. Jesse gets inside and closes the door. They settle into the warmth and comfort of the wagon.

"All set, then?" Mrs. Sharky asks and without waiting for an answer she puts the car in gear and takes off. After they pull out of the high school parking lot, Mrs. Sharky wonders out loud "How was the dance?"

"It was good, mom." Dawn replies.

Enthusiastically, Jesse adds "It was great, Mrs. Sharky. Dawn really knows how to dance."

"Oh? That's nice." Mrs. Sharky replies with just a little bit of snippiness and that ends the conversation. They ride in silence for a few blocks, but all the while Jesse is thinking about how awesome the night has been, going on a date, dancing with Dawn, even helping her with the clean up stuff. He's been back in America just a short time and he has already had just about the best night of his life.

Out of nowhere Jesse blurts out "This is the biggest car I've ever been in. It's gigantic!" That brings a small laugh from both Mrs. Sharky and Dawn. In a much more lighthearted voice, Mrs. Sharky says "It is indeed a big wagon. Rex calls it our Land Shark."

Now Jesse laughs and says "That's funny. I like it."

A minute later Mrs. Sharky stops Land Shark in front of Jesse's house. Jesse says thanks to her and reaches for the car door.

Dawn offers "Let me walk you to your door" and slides out the same door as Jesse. Jesse likes that she did that, rather than go out the other side of the car. He helps her out and together they walk.

Half way to his front door Dawn uses her best hillbilly accent when she says "Jesse Colton, ah sure had me uh nice time wid you t'night." Jesse plays along. With his own Dogpatchian accent he replies "Ah sure did, too Daisy Dawn Mae. Y'all dances real nice-like" They hold hands while they walk the last couple steps in silence. Jesse tries to figure out what his next move should be or if he even has a move. When they stop at the front door Jesse looks into Dawn's eyes and so wants to kiss her. She looks like she wants to kiss him, too, but he's afraid to klutz things up. He's never kissed a girl. What if he does it wrong? Runs into her nose or tucks in his lips rather than puckers? What if he kisses her like he kisses his mom? No matter, he decides he has to try.

Jesse begins to lean towards Dawn. He sees her lean towards him. Just as their lips are about to touch Jesse closes his eyes. As he does so, he looks from Dawn's lips to her eyes. He sees she is just beginning to close her eyes, too, but already only the whites are visible.

When their lips first touched, it was simply the physical contact for Jesse. It was good. It was fine. It was more than he had hoped for but then something unexpected happened. Even though they had moved closer together, it wasn't the press of her body as she hugged him or the warmth of her arms around him. It wasn't even the continued press of her lips on his. Jesse took all this in and was excited by it. As her kiss lingered, she opened her mouth just a little bit and that's when he felt the change begin. Her soft exhale carried faint, yet familiar, vapors. Vapors that heightened his senses and triggered memories.

This was his first kiss, what memory could it possibly trigger? He had no other kiss to compare it to. As Jesse is holding Dawn, kissing Dawn, the image that pops into his mind is of a warm, steaming bowl of soup. It's Mrs. Lee's shark fin soup, sitting on her table, waiting, calling for Jesse to dig in.

The image had suddenly and unexpectedly appeared to Jesse ,but without regret or a second thought, he kicks it out of his mind. Dawn is here. Dawn is now. He pulls her closer and kisses her with more passion. This is bliss for Jesse. He could stand here with Dawn, in the soft porch light, until the next morning's sun arrives.

Unfortunately, there is the inevitable beep of a car horn. After that, Dawn slowly pulls back from Jesse, letting go with her arms and then with her lips, but not with her eyes. She looks at Jesse with great intensity, as if she is trying to drill into his mind and read his thoughts.

There is another beep of the horn. Dawn's expression transitions to more of shy smile, then she says "My mom was watching us".

Jesse smiles and replies "I hadn't noticed"

Dawn's smile brightens at his comment. Then, back in her hillbilly voice, she says reluctantly "Ah betta git going. Ma's awaitin' fer me." She continues with "Jesse Colton.." but then she pauses and takes a step backwards, towards her mom's car. In her normal voice, Dawn says "see you on Monday", and without waiting for a reply, she turns, and dashes to the Land Shark and gets in.

Jesse watches the Land Shark until it disappears into the murky November darkness. As warm as he feels on the inside, the coldness of the night is catching up to him. He turns and reaches for the door knob. Inside, Jesse closes the front door. As he walks towards his bedroom he says to himself "I just kissed … the strangest, most interesting girl I've ever met." After another step and half he adds "I like her…more than shark fin soup."

Three years later
This October, like Jesse's previous three Octobers in Bakersfield, is still hot. The calendar says its fall, but in Kern County the day time temperatures are more likely to peak over 100 degrees rather than eek up to only mid 60s. In this heat, Jesse is one of the few students at Bakersfield College to be wearing long pants. Along with his denim jeans, he is wearing tennis shoes, white socks, a black leather belts and a hunter green polo shirt which is neatly tucked in. He is the same good, solid, simple person, both in character and style, as when he arrived in Bakersfield.

He also has a backpack slung over his left shoulder. The pack appears to have at least three good size books inside. With his right hand he is holding Dawn's left hand as they walk from the college parking lot to the library. Dawn is wearing navy blue shorts, a light blue cotton top and strappy sandals. In her right hand she holds a single peechee folder and a thin workbook. They are both proudly wearing the cheap sunglasses they bought during their last trip to the Saturday morning flea market at the Sunset Drive-In Theatre.

Dawn starts to swing their holding hands in a happy motion. In a voice perfumed with playfulness she says

"You know...I'm thinking of becoming a dentist"

Jesse plays along, "Oh really? Why just yesterday you wanted to be an orthodontist and the day before that a dental hygienist. You seem to have a fascination...a fixation on teeth. Why is that?"

"Well..." She pauses as a big smile crosses her face. "I think it all started back in high school. My boyfriend, strange as this may sound, he actually thought I had shark's teeth." She chomps her teeth a couple times.

"I see. And because you are so in love with this guy you want to go into some type of dental profession?"

Dawn just giggles as they continue walking.

The kiosk just outside of the library is covered with all kinds of flyers; roommates wanted, cheap textbooks, note taking services, but mostly posters for various classic movies still popular on college campuses. As a way to raise funds, the clubs, sororities and fraternities show movies like Animal House, Rocky Picture Horror Show and Aliens at the auditorium.

Dawn pulls Jesse towards the kiosk as she says

"Let's see if there's any movie playing at the auditorium tonight."

"I've got a couple hours worth of statistics and civil engineering to get through tonight."

Dawn is studying the kiosk flyers and answers in a distracted voice "Campus movies usually don't start until 9 or 10."

"The sooner we get to the library the sooner we can..."

Dawn suddenly interrupts Jesse with a shout "Oh my God. It's playing tonight! That's so perfect!"

"What?" Jesse asks. Then, knowing her love of classics he asks "Casablanca?"

"No"

"Ten Commandments?"

"No"

"Monty Python and the Holy Grail?"

"No, not even." She lets go of his hand and says "It's..." and then uses both her arms to make a big chomping motions as she continues. "Dahn dah..dahn dah..dadadah..Jaws!"

"Oh, you are so funny. You are mega funny. What time does it start?"

"9:30"

"Okay, we can go see it if I can get my homework done before it starts."

"Well Jesse Colton, then you best get started."

Back to hand in hand, they head into the library.

Clyde

Yesterday I saw a baby coot.
It was barely the size of an oompa loompa's boot.

I said "Hey little fella, won't you come with me,
Where the river is chocolate. It's something to see!"

We headed back to my magic factory,
Cootie, me, and a scruffy possum, made three.

Already the kids were waiting for us
So we welcomed them in without much fuss.

We started the tour with the snotty little brats
And the first one to go was the one called Fats.

"He can't swim" his big mother exclaimed.
The buck-toothed possum whispered "Oh well, who's to blame?"

The rest of the squirts were each chucked aside
Until all was left was the cootie name Clyde.

I told him he won save for one misdeed.
When he swam in the river I'm sure he peed.

On his way out the door he left me a pellet.
I told him "Good day" and didn't need to smell it.

The factory is still mine and the loompas are here,
But we've given up on chocolate and switched to beer.

Made in the USA
San Bernardino, CA
10 May 2018